GRACIE
The Pixie of the
Puddle

GRACIE
The Pixie of the Puddle

DONNA JO NAPOLI

DUTTON CHILDREN'S BOOKS ✦ NEW YORK

Copyright © 2004 by Donna Jo Napoli

Library of Congress Cataloging-in-Publication Data
Napoli, Donna Jo, date.
Gracie, the pixie of the puddle/by Donna Jo Napoli.—1st ed.
p. cm.
Summary: When she realizes that her friend Jimmy can change from frog
to human and back again with aid of a magic ring, Gracie the frog tries to
find a way to persuade him to remain a frog permanently.
ISBN 0-525-47264-9
[1. Frogs—Fiction. 2. Magic—Fiction.] I. Title.
PZ7.N15Gr 2004
[Fic]—dc22   2003019227

Published in the United States by Dutton Children's Books,
a division of Penguin Young Readers Group
345 Hudson Street, New York, New York 10014
www.penguin.com

Designed by Gloria Cheng
Printed in USA · First Edition
1 3 5 7 9 10 8 6 4 2

In memory of my mother

ACKNOWLEDGMENTS

For feedback on earlier versions, I thank Lillie Dremeaux; Eleda, Marena, and Ted Fernald; Betsy Horner; Aongus O' Murchadha; Ben, Beth, and Margaret Murray; Erica Newbold; Lindsey Newbold; Richard Tchen; Jeff Wu; Chandra Yesitas. Special thanks go to Ed Gaynor's fourth-grade class at the Swarthmore–Rutledge School in 2001–2002. And for help on multiple drafts in all the thousands of usual and unusual ways, I thank my family and Lucia Monfried.

CONTENTS

GRACIE
The Pixie of the
Puddle

Close Call

I WAS NIBBLING at the dangling roots of pond weeds that bobbed on the water's surface, completely content. A frog's life is full of blissful moments, and this was one of the best. It couldn't have been a better day.

Jimmy swam past in a hurry.

An instant later a voice said, "Well?" It was a big male frog, swimming right behind Jimmy. "Now? Huh? Yes?"

Something was up. Yay, I loved excitement. And anything with Jimmy was bound to be fun. I swam after the two of them, straining to hear.

"Not now," said Jimmy.

"When?" said the male.

"Later," said Jimmy.

The big male stopped. His nostrils stuck out of the water, and the rest of him hung down like the pond weed roots. He seemed disappointed.

"Look out," shouted Jimmy.

That's when the water snake struck. He swallowed the big male whole.

I dove to the bottom. My heart fluttered. My skin quivered.

That frog was inside the snake's gullet. Still alive, for sure. But that was more terrible than if he were dead, because he knew there was no chance. Green frogs have no claws, no teeth, nothing to help fight their way out of a snake's innards.

The water roiled around me. The snake's tail spun fast. I gathered my strength to flee when—right behind the snake—I saw small, dark dorsal spots that formed the pattern I knew so well; Jimmy was following the snake. Why on earth?

He swam at the snake's underside and rammed his head below the bulging throat. The snake's whole body rippled from the blow. Jimmy swam at it again. Bump. The snake's head flung backward. And again, bump.

The snake opened his jaws, and the frog inside burst out and away, lost in the churning waters.

The snake sank slowly to the bottom.

I stared through it all. I'd seen frogs eaten by snakes before. I'd seen frogs eaten by turtles. But I'd never seen anything like this. "You killed the snake," I said.

"Come on," said Jimmy. "Let's tie him in a knot."

"Are you nuts? Even if he's dead, I don't want to get near him."

"He's just stunned," said Jimmy. "Hurry. We can teach him a lesson."

A lesson? The idea had a strange appeal.

We grabbed the snake's tail. Scales—ugh. The snake lifted his head to look at us groggily.

"Hurry," said Jimmy again, "before he gets his bearings."

We looped the tail through itself.

The snake seemed to finally understand what was going on. He yanked away.

We took off fast.

Once we were at a safe distance, we looked back. The snake came up and gasped for air. Then he disappeared back under in a mess of wild splashes.

Jimmy laughed. "Maybe next time he'll think twice before he swallows a frog."

Now I laughed, too. Jimmy had made a fool of a snake. Then the realization of all that Jimmy had done hit me. I stopped. "You're a hero," I said.

"For what? We tied him up together," said Jimmy. "Come on, let's go."

We swam toward the center of the pond. "That's not what I meant. You saved that other frog. That's why you rammed the snake, isn't it? To save him. You're a hero."

"No, I'm not. I wasn't in danger."

"Of course you were. Look how he swallowed that other frog whole."

"Exactly," said Jimmy. "That snake knew that if he opened his jaws, he'd lose the frog inside his throat. So he wasn't dangerous at all—not to me."

I thought a moment. "How did you figure that out?"

"Don't be dumb, Gracie."

Well, that got me mad. I'm smart. I had just figured out why Jimmy had done something that would have baffled any other creature of the pond. Plus, I'm sensible. I'd never have rammed the snake, even if I knew he couldn't bite me; frogs just aren't aggressive that way. "You know," I said, "we're not like snakes or turtles; frogs don't go on the offense. What made you even think of ramming into the snake's side?"

"Speed up," said Jimmy. "We're not far enough away yet. The snake will get free any minute now, and he's going to be furious."

I swam faster.

The big male appeared right then with a smile on his face. "Now?" said the big male. "Now? Yes?"

"No," said Jimmy.

"When?"

"Later," said Jimmy.

"You said later before," said the male. "So now is later."

"No," said Jimmy. "Later is later."

"Oh," said the male. He swam off, looking as disappointed as he had before the snake gulped him up.

"I bet he'll get eaten again," I said to Jimmy.

"I hope not." Jimmy rubbed his face. "I don't know if I can be a battering ram twice in one day. It hurts."

His face hurt? Jimmy could have quit ramming the snake as soon as his face started hurting—but he kept it up. He really was a hero. "That simpleton didn't even say anything about you rescuing him."

"He probably doesn't know," said Jimmy. "He was inside the snake when it happened."

I watched the big male disappear. What an empty-head. "Why does he keep asking you when? What does he want?"

"It's time for the Pin Impersonator Festival, and I'm always the first performer. He wants me to start right away. But I need to practice my story more first. I want it perfect." He climbed up onto a lily pad.

Pin was an amazing frog who lived in this pond two summers ago. He was the father of Jimmy and forty-nine other frogs who called themselves the fawgs. I never met him, but I'd heard a lot about him. He talked funny, and the festival performers impersonated him as they told about his legendary deeds. Jimmy was the best at Pin talk.

And he obviously knew it. He extended his throat in pride now.

I couldn't take my eyes off that beautiful throat. It was pure yellow, like every adult male green frog's throat. Jimmy wouldn't be full-size until the end of the summer, but he was mature. He was adult.

That meant I was, too, because we hatched in the same spring. I didn't feel adult, though. I felt playful. "Hep! A nake! Hep!" I screamed in Pin talk, and I thrashed around, pretending a snake had gotten me and I needed help. "Hep me, hep me."

Jimmy lassoed my forefoot with his tongue and pulled me onto the lily pad beside him. He grinned.

I should have grinned, too. Yet somehow in this moment I felt something strange and new. I sneezed. I sneeze when I'm confused.

Jimmy looked at me. "What's on your mind?"

Nothing was on my mind. I suddenly couldn't think.

"Want to skitter?" Jimmy dove and swam toward our special area of shore. I zoomed with him. After all, nothing was better than skittering. We climbed out of the water at the same time, exactly synchronized. The ground along this section of the shoreline was firm, and there was hardly any underbrush, so we could start from way back and not get slowed down.

"Ready?" said Jimmy.

"At the same time?" Usually we took turns.

"Why not?" Jimmy's skin glowed, as though his body was lit up from inside.

All frogs are attracted to light, of course. But this was more than that. Jimmy really was the most handsome frog in the world. I nodded.

"Ready, set, go!" called Jimmy.

We leaped as fast as we could toward the pond; then we bounced together across the surface of the water in a series of rapid jumps until we finally plunged under.

"Skittering is the best," I said, as we came up.

Jimmy laughed and splashed me.

I splashed back.

A Chance

HOOFBEATS.

That meant a horse.

And a horse meant the prince.

I headed due east and stopped as soon as the big iron rock on the muddy bank came into view. I waited, letting the water bob me along, confident that I could see and hear everything important from this spot.

The nostrils and eyes of other frogs stuck out of the water here and there around me, none any closer to the shore than me.

Well, that wasn't completely true. One frog bobbed within leaping distance of the mud. I was pretty sure it was Jimmy and that he'd swim even closer to shore when the horse appeared. He had a thing about horses, after all. And ever since last summer, when he'd visited the palace, he'd had a thing about that prince, too.

The giant horse Chester came trotting up. The prince was riding him. Jimmy was right, I had to admit: Chester was a magnificent beast. In the fall, the prince used to ride Chester to the pond often. But then we went into hibernation, and now was the first time this spring that I'd seen him.

I'd actually ridden on that horse last summer. I'd felt the speed of his gallop. At the time, it was terrifying. But in retrospect, it was thrilling. So when I looked at Chester now, tingles of pleasure ran through me.

The prince jumped off Chester's back with youthful agility. Now that surprised me.

Last summer the prince had been a young man. So by this spring, he should have aged into full maturity. After all, that's how green frogs do it. The first summer, we grow from tadpoles to froglets. The second summer, we're youngster frogs. The third summer, we're young adults. The fourth summer, we're mature adults. The fifth summer, we're on the waning side of middle age. The sixth summer, we're positively old. After that, we're decrepit. All that, of course, is if we actually live that long. There are so many dangers in a frog's life.

So by now, one year later, the prince should have been a mature man. Instead, he still looked young.

The prince paced along the shore. He circled the big iron rock a few times. "Are you there?" He stopped and looked out over the water. "I can't stop thinking about you. At first I missed your mother. But that couldn't go on. We're just too different. And I've got a human wife now. Can you understand that?"

He picked up a stone and wiped off the caked mud. Then he skipped it across the water.

"Now it's you—you're the reason I come back to the pond." He shook his head sadly. "I miss you." His voice caught. "I meant what I said, what I always say. Come live with me. All of you." He chuckled softly. "Imagine that, the palace overrun with my children. Wouldn't that be great?"

He rubbed his palms. Then he stopped and held his hands quiet in front of his chest, palms together. "You're not like the rest of the pond creatures. There's a whole other life waiting for you. A life that would suit you better." He chewed on his bottom lip. "If you're as old as I think you are by now, it's time for you to make a family. Don't do it in the pond. Because if you do, you'll never want to leave. I know. Give me a chance first. Come see what I have to offer."

He squatted at the water's edge and looked at one spot. His hand shot out fast, and he plucked a sow bug from a lily stem. He popped it in his mouth. "For old times' sake," he said, and chuckled again. Then he got on Chester. "Think about it. You have a choice." He left.

Almost immediately the frogs around me disappeared. The show was over. And what a show it had been. Complete nonsense. "Give me a chance"—well, he'd said that before. "You have a choice"—he'd said that before, too. And it was just as baffling every time. But the most ridiculous thing was that bit about "my children"—as though somewhere in this pond there were children of the prince.

He was addlebrained, poor thing. Humans really were a mess.

Oh, well. At least frogs could be counted on to act right. I was grateful for that.

I dug a hole in the mud bank and crawled in, hind legs first, to nap and dream about the upcoming Pin Impersonator Festival.

T H R E E

Stories

THE NEXT MORNING, frogs crowded on the mud-
flats on the south side of the pond with a fervor that
could mean only one thing: The Pin Impersonator
Festival had started. Jimmy was performing. And I
was missing it.

I swam as fast as I could and climbed out onto
the shore. Most frogs are bigger than me, which has
never bothered me—I can do anything a big frog can
do. But right now I wished I was huge so I could
see Jimmy over these other frogs' backs. I leaped
along the edge of the tightly packed group, catching
glimpses of him each time I went up. He looked
shiny and dazzling in their midst.

I leaped as high as I could toward the middle of the throng of frogs. *Thwack.*

"Oooof," said the frog under me.

"Sorry. Make room on the mud, and I'll hop off your head."

"Stay where you are," he said in a mature voice. "I like it."

"Thanks." I had a great view now. And I could hear everything.

"De hag gwabbed me in her gnawy fingerth," boomed Jimmy in that way he does near the climax of a story. "But I had to thave poow Jimmy, poow poow Jimmy, twapped in de bucket." He was pretending to be Pin, using Pin talk, and all of us could translate easily: *The hag grabbed me in her gnarly fingers. But I had to save poor Jimmy, poor poor Jimmy, trapped in the bucket.*

Oh, yay. This was one of my favorite stories. When Jimmy was just a froglet, he had been trapped in a bucket by the wicked hag who used to plague our pond. She grabbed Pin while he was trying to save Jimmy.

What a hideous witch. Last summer she even threatened to dry up the whole pond and kill us all. But she got tricked by her own crystal ring and turned into a huge lump of iron rock—the very rock the prince had stood beside yesterday after-noon.

I imagined Jimmy in that bucket. I'd have been frantic in his position. No frog can stand being cooped up. Why, I would have been doing flips in-side that bucket. Just the telling of it was so scary that I couldn't keep myself from doing a small flip right here. *Plip.*

"Hey," said the frog under me. "What are you doing? Oh, I know you."

I looked down and jerked back with a start. It was the same big male that the snake had swallowed yesterday. "Sorry," I said. "I got carried away."

"That's okay," said the male. "I liked it. Do it again."

This frog was a little weird. But his head was a fine viewing spot, so I sat tight and looked straight at Jimmy.

"I tode Jade to eap high," said Jimmy, louder than ever. That meant *I told Jade to leap high.* "'Eap at de bucket, Jade, eap, eap,' I thaid."

Jade was Jimmy's mother.

"Dat wath when de fowty-nine oder fawgs came to hep," said Jimmy. Oh, yes. *That was when the forty-nine other fawgs came to help.* The fawgs—that's what Jimmy and his siblings called themselves. His voice quaked with emotion. "Dey jumped at de bucket, wham, boom, and o-ve it went. Jimmy wath fwee. A fawg victowy."

A cheer went up from the fawgs.

But the rest of the frogs sat silent.

"Never," said the male frog under me. "Frogs would never do such a thing. He's psycho."

"I don't believe a word of it either," said the frog beside him. "Frogs don't help each other."

That was the truth—at least for most frogs. Sometimes a frog will make a distress call to scare off predators, sure. But we don't do it to warn other frogs. And other frogs don't come to the rescue.

Still, it was funny to hear the big male talk like that, given that he'd be history if Jimmy hadn't helped him escape from the snake. But, like Jimmy said, he didn't know what Jimmy had done. And if I told him, he wouldn't believe me. Just like no one believed the bucket story. He'd call me psycho, too.

If anyone other than Jimmy had been telling this story, the frogs would have slipped into the water and away at the first mention of Pin wanting to save his son. Frogs don't have time to waste on fools.

But no frogs left. They all stayed put and listened. Jimmy was such a good storyteller.

When Jimmy finished, he did a dramatically high dive into the pond and swam away. The crowd hopped off helter-skelter, as frogs will, until time for the next performance. I didn't go hopping off, though. I swam straight after Jimmy.

I caught up with him near the lily pads. The flowers weren't out yet, but the leaves were already thick and wide and inviting. I climbed onto one. "Good story," I said.

Jimmy floated by the edge of my lily pad. "They didn't believe it really happened. They don't believe that the forty-nine other fawgs knocked over the bucket. They never do."

"Of course not," I said.

Jimmy dove to the bottom.

I dove after him. We scooped up glass worms, gobbling until our bellies were full.

Jimmy squatted in the silt. "Do you?"

"Do I what?"

"Do you believe me?"

I thought of Jimmy ramming into the snake's belly yesterday. "All kinds of things are possible," I said.

Jimmy hopped closer to me. "Does that mean you do believe?" His front toes splayed far apart, and his body tensed toward me.

"Why do you care so much?" I asked. "You're a great storyteller, Jimmy. I love to listen to you. And not just at the Pin Impersonator Festivals. I love it even when it's just you and me, and you're telling the craziest tales."

"Which are the craziest?" asked Jimmy.

I thought a moment. "Well, the ones about things you did in the palace."

"They're not crazy. You went to the palace, too," said Jimmy. "You saw it all."

I did go to the palace; that much was true. Last summer when Jimmy left the pond to visit the palace, I followed him. It was impulsive on his part. Well, I guess it was impulsive on my part, too. But there's nothing wrong with that. Frogs are often impulsive.

"Sure," I said with a shrug. "I was curious, so I followed you. But I got caught by a crabby princess, and I never saw you again."

"Yes, you did," said Jimmy. "I was always there, Gracie. I'm the one who saved the pond and carried you back here."

This claim wasn't new. Jimmy had said the same thing last summer, right after I finally got back to the pond. It made me mad then. And it made me mad now. "Look here, Jimmy. Somehow the crabby princess got hold of the hag's crystal ring. Then I stole it from her. Then the palace kitchen boy caught me and stuck me in his pocket and rode that horse Chester back to the pond. I carried the crystal ring in my mouth the whole way. And since that ring was what turned the hag into a huge lump of iron, I was the one who saved the pond. Me. Me me me." I stopped to catch my breath. "You're just jealous."

"Are you finished?" said Jimmy.

"For now."

"Everything you said is right," said Jimmy. "But what you keep not getting is this: I was the palace kitchen boy."

He'd said that before, too. And each time it sounded more fantastic than the last time. I laughed so hard I almost gagged.

But Jimmy wasn't laughing. He looked totally serious.

This was more than my froggy brain could take. I thought I might pass out from the strain of it. I rose to the surface and climbed onto the lily pad again.

Jimmy climbed onto a neighboring pad. "Well?"

"Well, what?" I said. "If you talk nonsense, there's no point in talking at all."

Jimmy sighed. "All right. Then just tell me one thing. Do you believe the forty-nine other fawgs tipped over the bucket and saved me?"

So we were back to that. I thought of how the fawgs had cheered at that part of the story and how the frogs had shaken their heads in disbelief. But everyone stayed to listen for the rest. And it wasn't just for the excitement. Now I knew there was another reason we listened: Somehow, in some little froggy recess of our brains, we all wanted to believe Jimmy's stories. We wanted to believe that a father would worry about his son even when he was caught in the hag's claws. We wanted to believe that a mother would try to overturn a bucket to save her son even when the hag could easily snatch her up with those very claws. We wanted to believe that brothers and sisters would fling themselves against the bucket without heed to their own safety. It was all so unfroglike, but all so attractive.

"I want to believe it," I said.

"That's about the best I could hope for." A gnat flew right past Jimmy's nose, but he didn't even flinch. "And that's not enough." He looked straight ahead into the clear spring morning and didn't say another word.

It's That Time

I HOPPED ALONG the bank, sneezing in confusion. Jimmy's stubborn claim that he had been the palace kitchen boy last summer was eating away at me. It wasn't just having him steal the glory. It was the nagging feeling that something was wrong with Jimmy.

Nearby, the big iron rock that used to be the hag baked in the sun. I leaped in a circle around it, faster and faster, to use up nervous energy.

"Awe you teathing de hag?"

It took only a second to translate: *Are you teasing the hag?* The very idea stopped me in my tracks. I looked over my shoulder. It was that goofball male whose head I'd sat on during Jimmy's story this morning. He was obviously practicing Pin talk for his own performance in the festival.

He didn't come too close, and I knew why. The pond creatures were afraid of the hag-rock, because no one could predict what the hag might turn into next. There was no way I wanted to tease the hag.

I hopped toward the water and looked back at the hag-rock from a distance. It seemed huge and foreboding, and it gave me the creeps. I wanted comfort; I wanted Mamma.

Where was she? "Toodleloo," I said to the male, and I slipped into the water.

It didn't take long to find Mamma; she was sitting on an ordinary rock that jutted out of the water. I climbed up and sat beside her, immediately happy. Mamma had that effect on me.

A water strider picked his jerky way across the surface of the pond past our rock. I zapped him with my tongue and swallowed. Yum.

Mamma zapped the next two.

We sat in the full sun, digesting in contented companionship. Gracie and Mamma.

Mamma wasn't my mother. She was Jade, the mother of Jimmy and the other fawgs. But I hung around her even more than her children did, so I got to call her Mamma, too. Hanging around your mother is an unfroglike thing to do. But hanging around Mamma and thinking of her as sort of being my mother made me feel good.

I took a deep, satisfied breath and looked around. Frogs squatted on lily pads and rocks and logs. Frogs' eyes and nostrils bobbed on the surface of the water, while their bodies and legs hung suspended below. It was a perfect froggy day. Even the appearance of a painted turtle on one of those logs couldn't spoil the atmosphere, because it was clear the turtle wasn't hungry. He was only after the sunlight. He lay there in the sun. I felt lazy, too.

What was that? A female frog hopped from lily pad to lily pad toward our rock. I could tell from the ease of her leaps that she was strong. And young. And she weighed enough to make the lily pads shimmy as she bounded, so she was substantial. More substantial than me.

She landed on the rock in front of Mamma. "Are you Jimmy's mother?"

"Yup," said Mamma.

"I'm Gracie," I said to the female.

"Frogs don't have names," said the female.

That was true. Only fawgs had names. But Mamma had named me last summer. I loved my name.

"Anyway," said the female, "who cares about you?" She did a high jump and landed facing

Mamma. "It's spring—courting time. Do you know where Jimmy is?"

This jumpy female was right: For the next four months, frog eggs would float in lovely black masses through the reeds and cattails. She was talking about that—and she was talking about Jimmy—all in one breath. My skin shivered, like the top of the pond in a breeze.

"Well," said Mamma, "he might . . ."

"No," I said quickly. I didn't want this female jumping around Jimmy.

The female looked at me expectantly.

"I'm Gracie," I said stupidly.

The female gave a disgusted snort. She turned back to Mamma. "All his brother and sister fawgs play down at the other end of the pond—the courting end—with the normal frogs. But he's never there."

Mamma didn't say anything. Good for her. Still, this jumpy female was right: Jimmy wasn't acting normal.

"They say he listens to you," said the female. "I don't know why. Frogs don't listen to anyone. This whole fawg family idea is loony. But Jimmy's strong and good-looking, so I'm willing to overlook his odd ways and defective sac."

Defective sac? I knew what she was talking about.

The green frogs in our pond have two vocal sacs and use them both at the same time, but fawgs sing only with their left vocal sacs. Their right ones stay flat. "That's no defect," I said. "It's part of his charm." The instant I said it, I wished I could take it back. This female was the last frog I wanted to make aware of Jimmy's charm.

"Charm? You might want him 'cause he's charming. I want him 'cause he's strong."

"I didn't say I wanted him. Did I say I wanted him? I didn't say that." I turned in a circle on the rock so fast that I slipped off and had to scramble back up, spluttering. "I didn't say that, Mamma. She's jumping to conclusions. Look how jumpy she is."

"Suit yourself, Grackle," said the female.

"It's Gracie," I said. "Gracie, Gracie, Gracie."

But the female wasn't listening. "Well, old woman frog, just tell Jimmy I was looking for him." And she was gone.

A snail slowly worked its body up the bumpy fuzz of a nearby bulrush. I shot out my tongue and swallowed him. Then I spit him out again. I couldn't eat. Well, that made no sense. A sensible frog eats every time food passes.

Mamma ate my spit-out snail. At least it didn't go to waste.

"Think she's going to look for Jimmy?" I asked.

"Who cares?" said Mamma.

"Don't you? Jimmy's children will be your grand-children."

"It's not in my nature to meddle." Mamma ate another snail, one I hadn't even noticed. Maybe I was sick. "Why do you ask?" she said.

"It was just a question," I said quickly. After all, it wasn't in any frog's nature to meddle.

And where on earth did my question about grandchildren come from? Jimmy's tadpoles would hatch and go about their lives in solitude until they grew up and found a partner. Then they'd separate and go on in solitude until the next spring, and the next partner, if they lived that long. That was the way of the frog.

That was normal. And I was a normal frog.

On the other hand, ever since I had met the fawgs, I hadn't spent my life in solitude. The fawgs played games together and went on swimming adventures together and just generally enjoyed being a family. And they included me. So I hadn't been alone, un-like normal frogs.

And I hadn't found a partner. Yet.

I moved closer to Mamma. "Gracie and Mamma," I said out loud.

"Yup," said Mamma.

Inside my head, though, I was saying something

else: Gracie and someone. Gracie and who? Gracie and someone someone someone.

"Croak."

I tilted my head toward a high rock over in the shade. On top of it sat a mature male frog. And, wouldn't you know, it was that same goofball male. He had to be at least in the fourth spring of his life. Maybe fifth. He was a good survivor, though I didn't see how.

"Croak. Croak, croak, croak, croak."

That was definitely a courting song. I nudged Mamma. She hadn't paid attention to male frogs since Pin disappeared two summers ago. Maybe it was time for a change. "What do you think of him?"

"You're full of questions today," said Mamma.

"Croak, croak, croak." The male's vocal sacs were inflating and deflating as fast as a dragonfly flaps its wings.

"He's getting all worked up," I said. "Don't you think you should do something?"

"Like what?" Mamma stretched one hind leg out behind her leisurely. Then the other. She often basked in the sun that way.

"Well, tell him if you like him," I said.

"Me?" said Mamma. "He's singing to you, Gracie."

To me? I looked up at the frog again.

He croaked enthusiastically.

I hopped to the other side of Mamma, away from the croaker.

The male croaked louder than ever.

Mamma and I were in full sun, and it was the hottest part of the day, so we had paled to a light green in that nice way that frogs have of deflecting the heat. We hardly stood out from the background of moss in the crevices of our rock. But the male's high rock was shaded by an overhanging willow, so he was still a deep, brilliant green, not camouflaged at all. He cut quite a fine figure way up there. And I just bet that's why he chose to sit on that rock— so we'd look up and admire him.

"Should we hop onto a taller rock in the shade?" I asked Mamma.

Mamma pulled in her legs and squatted. "I'd never sit in the shade of that tree."

"How come?"

"The hag once jumped down from that willow and grabbed me." Mamma trembled all over. "That tree is bad luck."

The creepy feeling came over me again. I didn't want to think about the hag.

The male on the high rock croaked insistently.

"You don't have to hop on a high rock to give that male a better view," said Mamma. "He's obviously interested as it is."

"I don't want to give him a better view," I yelped. "I just want to be on his level. Look at him. He's sitting up there like he's posing for our benefit."

Mamma and I looked together.

"Croak," went the big male, turning to show us his regal profile.

At that moment a pebble flew straight at the big male's forehead and knocked him—*plop*—into the water. What an unlucky frog. First the snake, now a pebble.

Mamma and I dove for safety.

FIVE

Monster

"WHOOPEE!" CAME a shout from above the water.

Rows and rows of frogs huddled on the pond floor. We watched in horror as billows of stirred-up mud moved through the water toward the big rock where the male had been sitting. With each billow, the pond floor vibrated violently. Minnows scattered.

A giant foot rose out of the muddy billows and plunged back down. Then another. Oh, no! They were the cause of all the commotion. Feet on the bottom of skinny, hairy legs. I gave a gasp that let precious bubbles of air escape from my lungs. I couldn't see above its knees, because the creature was so tall the rest of it stuck out of the water. But I knew these were the limbs of something horrid— a human or a hag.

Jimmy darted past at full speed.

"Stop!" called Mamma.

He didn't even slow down.

"Oh me oh me oh me oh me," Mamma muttered.

All at once I knew what Jimmy was doing. The big male that had been sitting on the rock was probably knocked unconscious by the pebble. He would drown unless someone held his head out in the air. Jimmy was off to save him for the second time in two days.

Well, mercy, he shouldn't try such a thing alone. And if I knew that, then everyone knew that. So if the fawgs really did help each other, they would come to Jimmy's aid.

I waited for fawgs to go zipping past. None did. Then I remembered what that jumpy female had said: All Jimmy's brothers and sisters were down at the other end of the pond. They didn't know about the danger here.

Without thinking why, I swam like a fiend.

"Stop!" called Mamma.

In seconds I was lost in the dark of those muddy billows. "Jimmy," I shouted. "Jimmy, Jimmy, where are you?"

"Where are you?" came another voice from above the water. "Where did you go? You're my frog. Here, froggy froggy froggy."

I swam blindly, faster and faster, and . . . *smack.* My head smashed into something, and I slipped sideways to the bottom. A foot came down on my belly. Hot and heavy and huge. My back pressed into the soft silt, but the colossal foot pressed down with me. All the air in my lungs squished out.

"What's that slippery thing under my foot?" came the voice from above the water. The pressure stopped abruptly. "Is that my froggy?"

I tried to right myself, but I couldn't. The monster scooped me from the mud.

In a flash I was suspended in the breeze, upside down, caught around the middle. Dizzy and nauseated. All frogs like to keep their head uppermost. Almost as though the hand that belonged to the colossal foot understood, it turned me right side up. I squeezed my eyes shut, so I wouldn't see the monster's teeth.

"Oooo, you're such a cute one."

I sucked in air fast. Then I gave the call of a condemned frog: "Misery."

"And what a cute little noise," it said. "Hello to you, too."

And now I knew: This wasn't a hag. Hags understand animal talk. The only creatures who don't are humans.

I finally dared to take a look at the human's face. What? It was Sally, the crabby princess who caught me at the palace last summer.

But wait. The girl holding me was awfully young—middle-size. Last summer Sally was a middle-size girl, just like I was a middle-size frog then. So by this summer she should have matured to a young adult woman, just like I had matured to a young adult frog.

I sneezed. Something was wrong. This girl was ill.

And, oh, Sally lived in the same palace the prince lived in. And the prince was younger than he should have been, too. They were both ill.

She grinned. Her teeth came to sharp points. Last summer she hadn't been a frog-eater. Instead, she'd caught me to keep as a pet. But who knew what changes the disease might have caused.

I tried to wriggle free. Ouch. My belly and back ached terribly. I stopped moving and played dead. I let my eyelids droop just enough so she'd think they were closed, but not all the way, so I could still see what was going on.

"You're so tiny. A pixie frog. I like that. Whoopee." Sally held the skirt of her dress up around her knees with one hand and held me with the other. She wiped a lock of hair from her face and dropped her skirt in the process. "Oh, dear," she said, gathering up her skirt again. "Look what you made me do. My skirt's muddy. You're a naughty froggy. But then, I like naughty things. Double whoopee." That lock of hair fell back across her eyes. She dropped her skirt again and swiped at her hair, but with a now muddy hand, so mud smeared on her cheek and hair. It was as though she was turning into a mud monster right before my eyes.

And now I saw it: A ring hung from a string around her neck. I recognized it right off. It was the very ring I had carried back to the pond in my mouth last summer—the hag's ring. The hag's magic crystal ring. Last summer the prince had stood on the shore and said he'd keep that ring safe so that it didn't fall into the wrong hands. And Sally's hands were wrong hands; that much was clear. Sally had stolen the ring from the prince once before, and he'd gotten it back, but somehow she'd managed to steal it again.

"I didn't mean to squash you, you know," she said. "It just happened. If you're not dead, we can still be friends."

I wriggled weakly again, but Sally's grip was firm. I opened my eyes fully and looked around at the pond, so lush with yellow spring iris and flat-bottomed whirligig beetles skating on the water's surface. I thought of the hundreds of green frogs sitting on the pond bottom with fairy shrimp and cyclops and fish eggs floating around them. In a month the white and pink lilies would be out. The tadpoles would swim everywhere they weren't supposed to go, their little undulating tails propelling them along. Their disobedience seemed endearing in this moment. Everything about this pond was dear to me.

The deep voice of a distant bullfrog came in four blasts of a single low note. Ordinarily I'd consider that voice an ugly intrusion. Bullfrogs have been known to swallow green frogs. But those notes were part of the pond. And they might be the last noises I'd ever hear from this pond. My pond. My wonderful pond.

The nostrils of a frog peeked out from the water on the other side of the high rock. Jimmy was undoubtedly struggling to hold up the big male so that he could breathe until he came back to consciousness.

"Good-bye," I called bravely. "Good-bye, good-bye."

"Are you saying something again, froggy?" Sally put her face close to mine. "That was a cute little croak."

Well, I had to gulp at that. My whispery, hoarse cry of farewell was nothing like a croak. Only male green frogs croak.

"I'll bring you home and save you until Prince-Know-It-All's new moat is ready." Sally rubbed her nose. It now looked like a big glob of mud. She shook her head, and mud flew from her hair onto the crystal ring around her neck. "Phooey! My ring's muddy now, too." She used the edge of her skirt to rub the crystal clean. Then she happened to glance up. "Oh, look!" She stared ahead over the water.

But I was looking at the crystal in the ring. It had started to shine amber when she rubbed it. Now it positively glowed, though Sally hadn't seemed to notice.

"Ah," she breathed, "ooo."

I looked from the crystal ring to what had drawn her attention.

A snake wiggled side to side through the water toward the bank, his head sticking up high into the air. It was the same snake that had caught the male frog the other day. The same snake Jimmy and I had tied a knot in. Why on earth? He was old enough to know better than to come out when there was trouble. Snakes have no ears, so he couldn't hear Sally talking. But he should have sensed from the vibrations in the water that something big had come through. How could he let his curiosity get the best of him like that?

But now I saw what he was after: a newtling on the bank. That snake was just a fool for a good meal.

The newtling stupidly munched on pond weed, unaware of the impending danger. He should have been eating potato bugs under rocks, like other newts. Something was wrong with him, and now he was going to pay for it. That's how the world worked—poor little newtling.

The snake slid onto the bank and rose to strike. Finally, the little newt saw him. He could never run out of striking range fast enough, and he knew it. He stood tall on his hind legs and curled his tail up behind him, showing the bright orange of his underside. He was trying to look ferocious. This newtling actually thought he could scare off a snake. Pathetic nitwit.

The snake rose higher, ready for the strike. And . . .

Sally lunged. "Got you." She held the snake up by the neck and laughed. "A frog and a snake. Whoopee, whoopee, and triple whoopee!" She danced around, shaking us and splashing wildly. "Ha! I thought I was going to catch only one creature today, but I already have two. It'll be easy to stock that moat."

The snake looked about in mute confusion. He

gave a sigh of dismay as he saw the newtling jump into the water and disappear. Then he spied me. His eyes gleamed.

"Don't get any ideas, One-Lung," I said to him, "or I'll tie you in a knot again."

The snake didn't flinch. Oh, of course not. He couldn't hear a word I said. His tongue flickered out and in again.

And this idiot was going to be my moat mate.

Sally was positively demented.

"I'm so happy happy happy," she sang, twirling along the shore. "Who knows what else I can catch to put in the prince's new moat? Maybe even a crocodile. Ha. It would serve him right, Prince-Know-It-All." She twirled past the hag-rock. "I wish this big old rock was a crocodile right now."

In an instant, a gigantic lizardlike, big-toothed monster stood on the mud where the hag-rock had been. It looked stupefied. Then its eyes lit like fires. Those eyes alone filled me with terror. "I'm a crocodile," it bellowed. "Yuck! A revolting croc! And that's my ring! My ring! My ring!" It charged Sally.

She screamed and squeezed so hard, my world went black.

The Pot

EVERYTHING WAS TUMBLING, and my middle hurt like mad. My head hurt, too.

Yikes! A snake swung by.

And now I remembered where I was. Sally pumped her arms as she ran, swinging me and the water snake, forward and back, forward and back. Every time her hands reached the bottom of the swing arc, I'd get a glimpse of the snake passing on the other side of her. He looked as wigged-out as I felt.

My body turned darker and darker green as my mouth filled with bitter bile. And I knew that there was something really bad gnawing at the back of my brain—something more dreadful than Sally and her plans—what was it? Her grip was so tight around me, I couldn't think straight.

After a while I closed my eyes and let the rhythm of her run send me into a trance, almost like the torpor frogs enter when the weather turns cold.

Pretty soon she slowed down. "That big croc gave up following us, thank heavens," she said. "I'll send servants back to catch it."

My stomach lurched at the mention of crocs. The image came back in a terrible jolt: a huge crocodile, running right at us with those raging eyes. It screamed, "My ring." But the ring that hung from Sally's neck was the hag's ring, not any gross croc's ring.

Unless . . . oh, no! The hag had changed shape again—she had turned from an iron rock into a crocodile. The ring had done its magic again.

"Mistress Sally, run!"

I looked around for the source of the voice. Up ahead was the palace Jimmy and I had visited last summer. And there was that same old cook, Kate, standing by the open kitchen door, shouting and waving.

"Is the crocodile after me again?" screamed Sally, breaking into a run.

"Yer imagination has gotten the better of ya," called Kate. "Crocodiles don't live in these parts."

"Yes, they do." Sally looked back over her shoulder and tripped, slamming the snake and me on the ground—*sploof!* My middle still hurt from where she'd stepped on me in the pond, and now my head hurt, too. Everything about being with this girl was a harrowing experience. She got up and limped. "I saw one."

"Don't be silly," said Kate. "Go change into something fresh right fast. The coach is waitin' on ya. This is the monthly outin' to the prince's family palace."

"I don't like the prince's family," Sally muttered.

"What did ya say, Little Miss? Don't be sayin' nasty things. Be a good lass and clean up. See and I've got a sweet bun 'ere to make yer journey not so tedious."

"I don't like Prince-Know-It-All, either," Sally said a little louder. She limped up to Kate, holding both hands out before her. "All right, the croc will have to wait. But look what I've got, Kate."

"A frog and a snake." Kate put her hands up in front of her chest as though to fend us off. "And what're ya plannin' with those, Miss?"

"They'll go in Prince-Know-It-All's moat," said Sally.

"You mustn't call 'im that. Just say 'prince' like everyone else. And that moat's not finished yet."

"It will be soon. The next time it rains, it'll fill up, and my froggy and snake can play. And the croc can rule the whole moat."

"Mistress Sally, there are no crocs around 'ere. But if there was a one, your father the king would send out a huntin' party to kill it."

"Not my croc. It's ugly and mean, but it's mine. Forget I said anything."

She went past Kate into the kitchen. "Get me a pot."

Kate looked askance at us, but she put a colossal pot on the floor.

Sally dropped in the snake. She plopped me down on top of him and slammed a lid on quick.

My brain stopped. I was in a pot with a snake. I sat motionless. The snake was equally still.

"Good," said Kate, her voice muffled by the pot lid, "now you 'ave to change clothes. That dress is a mess. And don't forget yer bonnet."

"I don't even want to go," Sally said. "It was better in the old days, before the wedding, when the prince would visit his family on his own, and we'd at least be rid of him for a few days. Now he drags all of us along. It's boring. He should take my prissy sister and go live at his father's palace. That's what princes are supposed to do—bring their brides to their home, not move in with the bride's family."

"Ah, now, don't go complainin' again. You've heard 'im say 'e's goin' to spend the rest of 'is life close to that pond you just got yerself all muddied up at. So hush now, and hurry or I'll be the one to pay the piper, 'cause they told me to find ya a half hour ago. I been searchin' and searchin'."

Running footsteps left the room, then came back. "Feed my snake and frog while I'm gone."

"Sure and I will," said Kate.

Running footsteps, away and then back again. "And when you go outside, be careful you don't get eaten by . . . well, by anything."

"Whatever ya' say, Little Miss," said Kate.

More running footsteps. Away. This time they didn't come back.

Silence.

Gradually my brain came awake again. Frogs don't see well in the dark. But I got a glimpse before Sally put the lid on: I had landed about a third of the way down the snake's body from his head. He hadn't moved since he got dumped in this pot. Not even a muscle twitch. But he was alive. And as soon as he got over the shock of being here, he would realize he was still hungry, and food was sitting on his back.

I was dead.

A feeble voice inside me said, "Don't be dumb."

It was as though Jimmy was inside my head, talking to me. It made me mad, and I started to think hard. My only chance was to locate myself somewhere this snake's mouth couldn't reach.

I took a teeny hop toward his head.

The snake didn't move.

I took another.

A muscle rippled under me.

I took another.

The snake's whole body tensed. My hops were resuscitating him. I had to do it fast, or I'd be snake meat.

I hopped madly up his back.

The snake twisted his head over his shoulder and showed sharp fangs in a quick snap of the jaw.

But I was already at the back of his neck, with all four legs clamped around his throat.

He threw himself around in the pot, slamming against the sides and lid, trying to knock me off. Slam, bam, smash. Finally he gave up and curled in a wide ring twice around the edge of the pot. He turned his head as far as he could and stuck out his forked tongue to try to locate me. The two tips tickled my side.

How long could I last like this? My legs were strong—any frog's are—but between the scales of this snake and my tight, slick skin, the chances of me holding on for very long were slim. For the first time in my life, I envied tree frogs their loose belly skin, which allows them to cling.

One side of the lid lifted slightly. Kate's big eyes peeked in. "And what are ya doin' in there? Sounded like a battle."

"Croak."

"Now where's that comin' from?" said Kate.

My question exactly.

"Croak croak croak."

"What . . . ?" squeaked Kate as Jimmy, my wonderful croaker, landed on her head. Kate tumbled backward onto her bottom with a loud "Ooof."

The pot tipped, and the lid went flying. The snake rolled out, me still tight to his neck. Jimmy jumped from Kate's head to the floor, then leaped in a huge circle around us.

This was the moment of escape; anyone could see that. Anyone but this daft snake. He went circling after Jimmy.

"Can't you think of anything but food?" I cried out, which was truly daft, since he hadn't grown ears in the time we'd been in that pot together.

"What?" said Jimmy.

"I'm not talking to you," I said.

The snake slithered all wobbly, but he kept after Jimmy doggedly.

Jimmy leaped faster. "Get off that snake."

"If I do, he'll catch you."

"I'm the one rescuing you," said Jimmy, "not you rescuing me. Get off."

"Out!" shouted Kate. She opened the door and grabbed a broom. "Out, out, out!" The three of us were swept outside, frogs and snake in a writhing mess.

SEVEN

The Coach

I JUMPED TO Jimmy's side. "Where is he?"

Jimmy pointed with a flick of his head toward the snake on the far side of him.

The snake had gathered into a tight coil, as though preparing to strike. He lay there, immobile. Then all at once he lengthened out and took off fast, straight for the pond. Water snakes have an uncanny instinct for finding water. Almost as good as an amphibian's.

And that made me realize how dangerously dry my skin had become. Frogs can't control evaporation through our skin—unlike dirty, bumpy toads. I looked at Jimmy. I could tell he needed water pretty bad, too.

I made a long leap and looked back over my shoulder. "Come on, Dreamer," I called, using Mamma's favorite nickname for him.

"This way," said Jimmy. He hopped under a bush.

Had he lost his sense of direction? "The snake went this way," I said coaxingly, trying not to embarrass him for not knowing what any frog should know. "Our pond must be this way."

"Our pond's too far. And the hag-crocodile is stalking out there. We'll go to the well in the garden beyond this hedge." Jimmy leaped away with certainty.

Jimmy had figured out that the crocodile was really the hag. He must have seen the whole thing happen. I didn't know what a well was, but the mention of that crocodile jumbled my insides. I followed Jimmy.

Within minutes we were sitting on a curved stone wall looking down into clean water. Coolness rose from the water's surface. Jimmy was right: This was a good spot.

We dove in, and soon enough we were frolicking. A little while ago we had been in mortal danger. And the crocodile was still out there somewhere. But this well was delightful, and frogs just can't help being happy. I twisted and twirled, absorbing water through every part of my skin until my thirst was thoroughly slaked. Then I swam under and around and over Jimmy for the pure joy of it.

Finally I rested, letting myself bob along. Jimmy did the same. "Did you save the big male frog?" I asked. "The one that got hit on the head with a pebble?"

"Mmm-hmm."

"Did he understand what happened this time?"

"Nope. He never figures anything out."

What a dunce that big male frog was. "Well, I'm grateful to you. Thanks for rescuing me from the pot."

Jimmy turned a happy brownish green. "You're welcome. It was lucky I came along at that moment."

"Lucky? You mean you didn't follow me?"

"Well, sure I did. I followed all three of you. But when you split up, I tried to keep my eye on the hag-croc. I lost her, though. So I came looking for you." He climbed out onto a little ledge under the well lip. "And thank you, too."

"Me? For what?"

"You wouldn't get off that snake's neck because you thought that then he'd catch me. You wanted to save me, too, Gracie."

I did, didn't I? The idea flustered me. I dove to

the bottom of the well and sat there a moment. There was no explanation for what I had done. But I was glad I had done it. Glad to the point of being giddy. I came straight up, popping the surface with a little splash. Jimmy still sat there, as brown-green as ever. "It's good to see you happy again," I said. "You haven't been happy lately."

"I've got things on my mind."

I swam back and forth in front of him. "Like what?"

"Just things."

If he didn't feel like talking about it, that was okay with me. Frogs don't pry. "How'd you know about this watering hole?"

"I hatched here."

"You're kidding." I looked around. There wasn't enough food for the hundreds of tadpoles that would hatch from a spawning. In fact, the amount of moss growing on the inside of this well was pitiful. "What did all of you eat?"

"Remember, there were only fifty of us. Pin carried all the others to the pond. Then Mamma and Pin fed the fifty fawgs."

"They fed you?"

"It's a long story," said Jimmy. "You better go home."

"Aren't you coming?"

"No."

I climbed out on the ledge beside him. "It's pleasant here. I'll stay with you till you're ready to go."

"You go on," said Jimmy. "I have things to do. If I don't hurry, I'll miss my ride."

Ride? "What are you talking about?"

"I may be gone a long while," said Jimmy. "Tell Mamma not to worry." He hopped out onto the stone wall, then disappeared.

I felt abandoned. My whole body shivered. And I was more confused than ever. I sneezed and sneezed. It made no sense. Any sensible frog heads home after a scare.

"And, hey," called Jimmy, appearing back on the wall again, "watch out for that croc on your way home."

"Oh, no," I said, as the vile thought hit me, "what if the hag-croc has gone back to our pond?"

"She hasn't," said Jimmy. "All the hag wants right now is to get her crystal ring from Sally. She's close by, for sure. So just be careful as you leave the palace grounds—after that, you'll be safe. And . . ." Jimmy hesitated. "Stay well, okay? I mean that."

"I'll try," I said. After all, what else can a frog promise?

"Stay well for my sake," said Jimmy. He disappeared a second time.

That was a strange thing to say. I kind of liked it. Well, actually, I liked it a lot. I waited, wondering what he'd say next, but he didn't come back.

I hopped onto the lip of the wall and looked in every direction. By the time I spied Jimmy, he had already reached the kitchen patio. He leaped around the corner of the palace, out of sight. Now that was truly odd behavior. Dangerous behavior.

Everyone has a right to privacy; any frog knows that. Plus all my instincts were telling me to head right home. Anything could be lurking behind any rock. And almost anything could eat a frog. But if it was the other way around—if it was me that had acted bonkers instead of Jimmy—Jimmy would come looking for me. So it was up to me to find him, talk some sense into him, and get us both headed home again.

I leaped off the well wall and followed Jimmy's wet path around the side of the palace. Then I sat stumped. There was no trace of him. Jimmy had stopped dripping well water by then, so there were no tracks to follow.

In front of the palace stood a gigantic box perched on four circular pieces of wood, with spokes in the center. The box had a top on it and a door in the side.

I heard a man calling, "Sally, Sally. Get in the coach. We've got to leave." It was the prince. That box must be the coach Sally was supposed to get into.

"Neigh." And that was Chester.

Another horse whinneyed in response.

And, oh, Jimmy had said he needed to hurry, or he'd miss his ride. I leaped as fast as I could toward the horse noises. And then I stopped and watched.

Inside the open coach sat a young woman dressed in green and pink. It was the princess Marissa, from last summer. She should have become an old woman by now, like Mamma was an old frog. But there she was, the same as last summer.

The prince had barely aged. Sally had barely aged. Marissa had barely aged. Even old Kate the cook looked pretty much the same. The whole palace was ill.

The prince came around the side of that coach and climbed up to a seat on the outside, behind the horses. Sally came dashing out the palace door, tying her bonnet as she ran for the coach.

"Croak."

Jimmy hopped toward Sally. Had he lost all his remaining senses? I leaped after him as fast as I could. "Stop," I shouted.

Sally knelt down. "Whoopee! It's my froggy. He

got loose just so he could come with me. Good froggy."

What a total airhead. She thought Jimmy and I were the same frog.

She put out her hand.

Jimmy jumped into it.

EIGHT

Gone

THE HORSES PULLED the coach out of sight. I sat aghast.

Jimmy was gone.

He'd hopped right into Sally's hand. She hadn't grabbed him. She hadn't even swiped at the grass. He had come to her willingly.

It was inexplicable.

"'Ere kitty kitty kitty," called the cook, Kate, from somewhere far away.

Kitty! Now I remembered: A huge, furry, clawed thing called Cashmere lived in this palace. A kitty-cat. And that kitty-cat had a penchant for torturing frogs. Last summer Cashmere had hurt Jimmy's leg bad. I'd seen it all from my hiding spot in the plants on the kitchen patio. Then Sally had picked up Jimmy and kissed his boo-boo leg. That was the last I'd seen of my Jimmy at the palace.

My survival instinct kicked in. I was drying out, I was exposed to predators, and I was hungry. It was time for action.

I hopped toward the well.

"Eeeeyowwww!" came the high-pitched scream. Cashmere streaked past me, straight for the open door where Kate stood.

I looked in the direction the cat had come from, just in time to see a tail with stiff ridges swing side to side into the undergrowth. The hag-croc! It had reached the palace in search of Sally and the ring.

I hopped faster. There was the well wall. I flew over it and plunged in. Silence rocked me on the bottom of the well for a long time. When I came up, I gobbled gnats and a few early-season mosquitoes. Finally, I faced the facts. Jimmy was gone. There was nothing for me here, all alone. I had no choice but to go home.

I hopped out and headed to the pond. Evening formed around me in that crisp way of new spring. The drop in temperature slowed my naturally cold blood. I hopped more slowly. The darker and colder it got, the more vulnerable I became.

A flash of brown-red fur shocked me. A meadow

mouse gave a shriek as the weasel chomped down on it. I had to fight off a shriek myself. The weasel looked around in challenge for any other predator who might want to steal her catch.

I didn't dare breathe.

The weasel ran off with the mouse hanging from her jaw.

Well, that did it for me. I didn't have the nerve to keep traveling in the dark.

Off toward the direction of the setting sun was a stand of trees and a bramble of wild rosebushes. I hopped to the bramble and backed in, careful of the thorns. Then I dug a hole with my hind legs and settled in against the main root of a bush. With the exception of my nostrils and one eye, I was entirely covered.

I waited. There were so many happy things to think about. My frog instincts told me that. But somehow I couldn't remember a single one. After a while I slept.

An aphid crawled across my eyelid, announcing morning in the most intimate way. Without even shaking off the dirt, I shot out my tongue and ate him. Yummy. But now dirt covered my tongue. I broke out of the ground that had crusted around me overnight and filled my mouth with saliva. Then I spat out the dirt.

Eating the aphid before digging myself out had been a foolish indulgence. I couldn't afford to waste my bodily fluid on spitting. It was still a long way back to the pond. I sat under the edge of the rosebush and peered out at the world.

Finches clustered in the branches of a nearby oak. They twittered and twitched, but they weren't flying off, so there was probably no predator hawk in the air.

What there was in the air was the stench of skunk. All frogs hate skunks, of course, the greedy, waddly beasts. But the odor meant that something even bigger had threatened the skunk. The memory of the crocodile's swinging tail almost blinded me with fright.

Still, the longer I stayed under the rosebush, the longer I'd be out of water. I might as well fill my stomach and take my chances in the open.

That first aphid had been just a hint of good things to come, for the morning-sun side of the rosebush was crawling with them. I feasted.

Then I set out, alert for danger, especially any trace of the hag-croc. But the journey home turned out to be uneventful. By midmorning I took my last tired hops through the grass and stopped on the muddy bank of our pond.

The pond was even more beautiful than when I had left it yesterday—when I'd thought I'd never see it again. Delicious water striders did their angular, acrobatic act on the water's surface. A catfish nibbled at the algae along the shallows. A newly molted toad sat near a rock swallowing its old skin. At any other time I would have considered that an ugly sight—toads have never been the friends of frogs—but not now. The pond was doing all the usual things it had always done, and nothing could be better.

The leaves of the willow shook gently in the breeze, casting shadows that played silly games. But then I remembered: It was near that willow that Sally caught me yesterday.

I dove into the water, straight to the bottom.

Mamma swam toward me at that very moment. She took a spot beside me and didn't say a word.

I was glad Mamma had just happened to be there. Unless it wasn't pure accident that she was there. Maybe she'd been on the lookout for me?

Her inner eyelids were acting as goggles, naturally, but her outer eyelids were up, and I could see exhaustion in her eyes. She might well have been watching for me since yesterday morning.

For me and for Jimmy.

Oh, what if Mamma had seen the hag turn into the crocodile?

The sight of me returning without Jimmy must have cut her heart. But she didn't even give me a questioning look. She would wait until I was ready to talk.

Love filled me. Yes, that's what it was—that feeling I heard the waterbirds talk about when I hid among the rocks with Mamma—it filled me to the brim. Amphibians hatch without any guess that such strong attachment is possible. But here I was, a froggy, feeling this way.

I rose to the surface. Mamma rose with me. We took our places on neighboring lily pads.

"I'm okay," I said.

"Yup," said Mamma.

"Did you see the monster?" I asked.

"The crocodile?" said Mamma. "Yup."

I should have realized she'd know that creature was called a crocodile. Mamma listened carefully to the migrating birds talk when they stopped at our pond, so she knew all sorts of things about water life in other places, even more things than I knew. "It's really the hag," I said.

"Yup," said Mamma.

"Jimmy says it won't come back to our pond."

"Why not?" said Mamma.

"It wants to get its ring back from the girl who caught me."

"Ah, I knew I recognized that ring," said Mamma. "We'll be in real trouble after the hag gets it again."

Mamma was right; the hag-croc could come back later and do any number of terrible things with that ring. She could catch frogs for hideous poison stews. She could dry out our pond and kill us all. She could do any evil thing she wanted. And Jimmy wasn't even here to help. Oh, dear. "Jimmy might be gone a while," I whispered.

Mamma's chest swelled as she took a deep breath.

"Maybe a long while. He said to tell you not to worry."

"Frogs don't worry," said Mamma automatically. Then she took another deep breath. After all, it was obvious to both of us that her words didn't make sense; Mamma had been worrying since yesterday. She wasn't a fawg—only her children were—but she had some fawgy ways, and this was one of them.

And, almost with a feeling of inevitability, I realized I was worrying, too.

"Where is he?" she asked.

Frogs are forthright by nature, so I couldn't keep

myself from telling. "He went off somewhere with the girl."

"She caught him, too?"

"No," I admitted, "he hopped onto her hand by choice." I hopped onto Mamma's lily pad, even though it was small, and my added weight made it sink a little. After all, I knew she needed solace after hearing that.

"Then what happened?" she asked.

"They got into a thing called a coach, and horses pulled them away, out of sight."

"I know what a coach is," said Mamma. "The pond I hatched in was near a palace with coaches." She lengthened her back and sat taller. "Who else was in the coach?"

"An adult princess. An old king. And, up on a high seat behind the horses, a prince and some other man." A small greenish-black fly zipped past. I ate it.

"A prince," said Mamma slowly. "The same one who visits the pond on horseback and says muddled things?"

"That's him," I said.

"Jimmy has ideas about that prince," said Mamma. "He thinks that Pin and that prince are the same. It's hard to understand, but he believes the prince turned into a frog for just one summer."

And Jimmy thought that he had turned into a

human last summer. Jimmy, our sweet dreamer, had lost his mind; there was no doubt left. "The cook said something about the prince's family palace. So I guess that's where they were going. But I don't know where it is."

Mamma thought a minute. "I do."

"You do?!"

Mamma drummed her toes. "Oh me oh me oh me oh me."

"Where?" I asked.

"Jimmy told me Pin and the prince came from the same place. That means the prince's palace is near the pond I first met Pin in. The pond where I was hatched."

Grace

"CROAK, CROAK." THE big male was back on the high rock, posing as proudly as ever, practically asking for some girl like Sally to come along and hit him on the head again. He'd been eyeing me for the past hour. "Croak, croak, croak." You'd think he didn't have a brain in his head.

Well, I had a brain, all right, and it was working overtime. I inspected the bank for telltale signs of turtles. Then I leaped onto it and ate haphazardly from the black clouds of gnats hovering above the mud. I went over the same facts yet again.

Here was what I knew:

Jimmy went with Sally to the prince's family

palace of his own free will. But no frog would choose imprisonment.

And the hag had turned into a crocodile and followed Sally to the palace to get her ring back.

Those were the facts.

"Croak." The male took a giant leap onto the bank and followed me.

I glanced over my shoulder at him.

"Croak." The male hopped around me now. "Croak, croak." Not much of a conversationalist.

I slipped into the pond and filtered plankton from the water by passing it over my gills. This was how frogs fed when they felt lazy. I wasn't feeling lazy. But I was too distracted to keep catching gnats.

Pretty soon I realized I had company. This time it wasn't the welcome company of Mamma, though. And it wasn't that fool male, either. It was the jumpy female from the other day.

"What'd you do with Jimmy?" she said. "Everyone knows he left the pond with you, but now you're back, and he's not. So what's the story, Grackle?"

"It's Gracie," I said, looking her right in the eye. "Gra . . . ukk." I had swum straight into a tangle of lily stems, and I was hopelessly caught.

"Gracie, I know," said the female, swimming back and forth in front of me. "You've got a name, big deal." She laughed. "You don't look graceful no matter what your name is."

Mamma named me. I'd never asked why she chose that name. I'd been so pleased to be named at all—and *Gracie* has a wonderful sound. But it was true that I wasn't a totally graceful frog.

"Don't just hang there in the stems, clumsy dingbat." The female swam faster, back and forth in front of me.

I pulled and thrashed and finally freed myself. "Jimmy's going to be gone for a while. A long long long while."

The female ate a cyclops. "So long that summer will be over by the time he's back?"

"I wouldn't be surprised," I said.

The female ate another cyclops. "I can't afford to miss the whole season."

"There's a very fine mature male hopping along the muddy bank right now," I said. I didn't mention that about all he could say was "croak."

The female took off toward the bank.

I sneezed in confusion.

What that female had said was true. Jimmy had left the pond with me—and now I was back, and he wasn't. I was where I was supposed to be—in a frog's element—and he wasn't. He had rescued me from Sally. But if that were the only reason he'd gone to the palace, he would have returned with me. Instead, he had told me to return to the pond alone.

I went over the facts one more time.

Jimmy said the hag-croc would follow Sally to get the ring.

After she got it, there was no telling what she'd do—just like Mamma said, we'd be in real trouble.

If Mamma and I could figure that out, so could Jimmy.

And what had Jimmy said after he'd rescued me from the pot in Kate's kitchen? He said it was lucky he'd come along. Lucky. He had been following the hag-croc, really—she was the first thing on his mind then. And she was the first thing on his mind now.

Jimmy was on a mission. He was trying to find a way to foil the hag so that she couldn't come back to our pond and do something awful. He was after that ring! He had gone with Sally in the coach for a reason. Oh, yes, I was sure of it now.

I rose to the surface and scouted for Mamma. She was flopped over a rotted tree branch that protruded from the water. Her hind legs stretched behind her, soaking up the sun rays. Her forelegs hung free in the air. Her eyelids drooped. She was as relaxed as I was wound up.

I tickled the tips of her fingers.

Mamma quick pulled her legs in, ready to leap for safety.

"It's just me," I said. "Gracie."

"Oh." Mamma tightened herself into a neat squat on the very tip of the branch.

I hopped up behind her on the lower part. "Where's your hatchplace?" I asked.

"Don't go there, Gracie."

I had to go there. Mamma's hatchplace was near the prince's family palace. And that's where Jimmy had gone. "Where is it?"

Mamma turned sideways and looked out over the pond.

I sidled up the branch a little.

The jumpy female swam past with the big male beside her. The male gave me a quick "croak" as he went by.

I watched a water strider hungrily. He was, unfortunately, out of reach. By the end of summer I'd be full-size, and my tongue would be long enough, but not yet. "I'm going to your hatchplace, Mamma."

"You'd be better off to think like that male."

I didn't answer. Finally, I said again, "I'm going to your hatchplace."

"This is your first courting season, Gracie. Don't waste it. It could easily be your last." Mamma zipped out her tongue and flipped the water strider toward me.

I snapped it up in gratitude. I hadn't realized she saw me eyeing it.

"Here today, gone tomorrow. That's a frog's life." Mamma zipped out her tongue again and ate a water strider herself.

In a terrible rush all the parts of me responded to the undeniable truth of Mamma's words. I did think about courting. I even wanted to know my tadpoles. That was unfroglike. Absurd. But true.

And Jimmy must want to, too. How could he not? To be surrounded by swarming masses of tadpoles screaming, "Am I a frog yet, am I a frog yet?"—how could anyone not want that?

In a second terrible rush I knew something else. Jimmy's grouchiness lately was part of his need for a family. Yet he hadn't gone swimming in the courting end of the pond.

Why not?

The quiet question came: Who did Jimmy want for a partner?

Maybe foiling the hag-croc wasn't the only reason Jimmy went off in that coach. After all, he'd heard the cook, Kate, say the coach was going to the prince's family palace. Which just happened to be near the pond where Mamma hatched. Which was the same pond that Mamma and Pin first lived in together.

Perhaps Jimmy wanted a partner from Mamma's old pond. A partner who was more like Mamma. A partner who wasn't clumsy.

"Tell me something, Mamma." It was hard to ask, but I had to know. "Why did you name me Gracie?"

"It was natural," said Mamma. "It was your natural grace."

"But I fall off rocks. And just a little while ago, I got tangled up in lily roots. I'm not in the least graceful."

"That's not the only kind of grace." Mamma laughed. "You're curious. And you're brave. That's grace deep inside." She ate another water strider.

Energy gathered in my center—maybe in the very place I carried the grace Mamma talked about. "I'm going to your hatchplace," I said. "I'm going to find Jimmy."

"Full of grace," said Mamma, "but obviously empty of brains. Do you want me to change your name to Loopy? Think about finding a partner, Gracie."

"I am."

Mamma was silent for a moment. Then she said very quietly, "It's not hard to get there. I'll tell you the way."

Buster

THE PLAN MAMMA and I devised would get me to her hatchplace by the third night. I would travel each morning, arrive at some water, eat, and then sleep until the next day. That way I'd be traveling at my best, full of energy and food. It was a sensible plan. A good frog's plan.

The trouble was, I couldn't fall asleep the night before the start of the journey. Every part of me jittered.

Finally, dawn came and I set out, exhausted and bleary-eyed. My first job was to cross the woods at the south of our giant pond. The thick trees gave a pleasant shade, and the pine needles underfoot were springy. Things seemed good, despite my sleepless night. In fact, the biggest problem was keeping myself from eating. Mamma and I had agreed that I should stay alert and wait until I reached my resting point for the night before having a meal.

Onward. To the other pond. To Jimmy.

I leaped like crazy over tree roots and around raspberry canes, leaped and leaped and leaped. Finally, I heard the song of the brook Mamma had told me about.

Fish gleamed silver. Somewhere along here was the bridge that I was supposed to sleep under tonight. I had reached my first day's resting place, and food, at last.

I jumped into the water and let the current carry me until I saw the bridge. I scrambled onto a rock. Ferns stuck out of the embankment. It would be a safe place to sleep.

Time to feast.

I waited.

And waited.

No insects flew by. No plants grew in water this swift, so there were no yummy slugs or snails crawling up stalks.

The sun was only midway through the sky.

If I stayed here, I'd be too hungry to travel tomorrow.

I leaped from the rock to the bank, crossed the

bridge, and kept going. After all, frogs are flexible: We make do.

The meadow was exactly how Mamma had described it. Blue bachelor buttons. Yellow Saint-John's-wort. Red poppies. I wended a path through the greenest parts, so I wouldn't stand out from the background if a predator passed. But even in the grasses, the sweet smells from the flowers wafted over and intoxicated me.

I watched intently for the bushes that would signal the location of my next planned stopping point: a small pond. I had originally planned to spend my second night at that pond—but now, instead, I'd spend tonight there. I hopped along happily.

Hours passed. Maybe I had veered off the path somehow.

"Croak."

Oh, welcome croak, though the male, whoever he was, sounded weak and weary. I listened for the chorus of all the other males of the little pond. But I heard only this one wobbly fellow. I followed his croaks and came to an area of reeds.

"Croak," said the male, hopping toward me with a pronounced limp. "Wowie. You'll do fine."

"Don't get any ideas," I said quickly. "I'm passing through for the night only. Where's the pond?"

"You're looking at it, baby."

"This? This is hardly a mud hole."

"It was an unusually dry spring," said the male. "With a little summer rain, it'll be perfect. And in the meantime, there's room for us."

"Whoa, Buster." I hopped through the reeds and ate four slugs just like that. Mud creatures have always been my favorite food. "Where are all the other frogs?"

"Most of them dried out over the winter. But those that woke in spring left for bigger ponds. You know how little loyalty youngsters have these days. They'll leave their pond at the slightest problem."

"Frogs often migrate in spring," I said. "They look for good breeding spots."

"Is that what you're doing? I didn't mean to insult you. You're obviously a thoughtful youngster."

I hopped along the mud, eating snails and slugs as fast as I could get them down. These reeds weren't such a bad place, really. That's when I saw them: crocodile prints. "Yikes, the monster was here."

"What?" The male limped over and sat in a print.

"You're sitting in a footprint," I said. "Don't you see it?"

He splayed his legs out, obviously trying to take up as much room as he could. "There's just me here."

Now I was suspicious. "Are you trying to hide that print?"

He scratched his toes around wildly, messing up the outline of the print. "This mud is super for making designs in," he said.

"You've got mud for brains if you think I'm fooled," I said. "That's a croc print. So where is it? Where's the monster crocodile?"

"Croco-what?" he said. "Maybe you suffer from nightmares. A lot of us do, you know. I won't hold it against you."

"You didn't dream it, Buster. It's a real monster. Called a crocodile. Where is it?"

The male hung his head. "It came yesterday and ate my only remaining companion. But it got a few snakes, too." Then he looked up hopefully. "Whatever, it's gone now. It's already come and gone. So this pond is totally safe."

"Fat chance," I said. "It could come back anytime." Still, the hag-croc would have to be really hard up to come back here. There wasn't enough life of substantial size in this mud hole to make more than a light snack for that monster. I hopped past the old guy and ate a few more slugs. "So you're all alone now?"

The male hobbled behind me. "What do we care who else is here and who isn't? We've got you and me, and it's spring. That's all that matters." He leaped and landed in front of me, tumbling onto his side. "Ooof. Boy, those leaps really take it out of you, don't they?" He settled into a proper squat. Then he stretched the leg that seemed to be giving him trouble.

"Who were you expecting?" I asked.

"What?"

"I heard you croaking. Who were you expecting?"

"No one," he said. "I was only hoping. I've been hoping every night this spring. And now I've got you."

This guy was the worst sad sack I'd ever met. I tried to break it to him easy: "I have no intention of staying here. I'm a traveler."

"Aren't they all?" he said wistfully.

Well, no wonder. No able-bodied frog would stick around here any longer than it took for a quick meal. "What happened to your leg?"

"It's nothing," he said. "Nothing at all. I'm strong. My offspring will be strong. Croak!"

"I'm not interviewing you for a partner, Buster," I said. "I just wondered about your leg. It was an innocent question."

The male looked at his leg and seemed to be trying to figure out an answer, as though the leg itself would tell him.

I looked, too. "That's quite a scratch." It ran practically the full length of his leg.

"The crocodile didn't do it," he said.

I believed that. If the hag-croc had come after him, he'd be digested by now. "Did you fall?"

"How did you guess?" he said way too fast.

"From where?" I asked.

"Why don't you guess that, too?" he said, this time way too hopefully.

"You're lying," I said.

"How can a question be a lie?" he asked.

Well, he had me there. "Did you fall or not?"

"I did fall. Yes, yes, indeed, I did fall. Wop! Splat! Ooof! It was awful."

"Then why did you act like you were lying?" I asked.

"You're persistent," he said. "I like that in a female frog."

"Buster, if you won't talk straight, I'm out of here," I said, which I shouldn't have said, since I was out of there no matter what. That swim in the brook at midday hadn't satisfied me at all. A frog needs to soak gently, not be swished around in currents. I was determined to get to a real pond by nightfall. And with all these slugs and snails in my belly, I felt sure I had the energy to do it.

"Okay, okay," he said. "Let's not do anything rash, now. I acted like I was lying because I felt like I was lying. Yes, that's it. That's absolutely it."

"You talk nonsense," I said. Something glistened between two reeds. It turned out to be a huge glob of dragonfly eggs. Ah, dessert. A few zips of the tongue made quick work of them. "Bye now." I hopped away.

"No," he called. "I'll tell you what happened. It was an owl."

I stopped. Owls were scary. "Go on."

"I watch out for predatory birds. I do, I do. I'm very good about avoiding them. My offspring will be, too. You can count on that. But this owl came at night, and I made the mistake of not burrowing down early enough. You know how hard it is to see wing shadows at night?"

"So what happened?" I asked.

"He got me. But I leaped when I saw him, so he only got me by the hind leg. I struggled like a champion, oh, you should have seen me, thrashing and throwing myself about side to side. And I used my secret weapon."

"Frogs don't fight," I said. "Frogs don't have weapons."

"Quite right," he said. "My secret weapon just sort of happened, you might say." His head bobbled with the excitement of his mysterious weapon.

"All right, already, what's your secret weapon?"

"I spit up on him."

"You what?"

"I vomited on him. Projectile-like. All over his breast feathers."

"Listen, Buster, vomit's not a weapon."

"Well, it should be," he said. "It worked. The owl dropped me. And I landed back in this pond."

"Mud hole," I said. "If it was a pond, you would have gone splash, not splat." Despite my attitude, though, this guy's story moved me. "Why'd you feel like you were lying?" I asked gently.

"I didn't get scratched by the fall—or even by the owl." He looked away in embarrassment and whispered, "I was in such a rush to burrow down into the mud, I didn't pay attention to an ordinary little stick. It turned out to be sharp. I can be clumsy that way."

Clumsy. He said *clumsy.* How could I possibly abandon him now? "Come on, Buster, let's get out of this dump and swim in a real pond tonight."

He didn't budge. "You know, I like the way you keep calling me Buster. It feels good."

He was right. I had named him—what a remarkable thing—I had named him like Mamma had named me. And the name suited him, like my name suited me. The wonder of it all made me happy. "You can call me Gracie."

"Gracie. That's a beautiful name. I'll remember

you when you're gone. Oh, yes, Buster will remember Gracie. All alone with nothing but a memory. No tadpoles for comfort."

"Stop that. You can't make me feel sorry for you. Besides, I'm not going anywhere without you."

"Yes, you are," he said. "I hop too slow. And I don't even know where the next pond is."

"I do," I said. "I've got detailed directions. I'll help you get someplace you can have a decent life."

"You'll help me?" he asked in astonishment. "What do you mean by that?"

I looked at Buster in equal astonishment. What was happening to me? First I named him; now I wanted to help him—like I wanted to help Jimmy. "Just get hopping," I said.

ELEVEN

Conversations

I USED TO think *slow* meant the way snails move or turtles think. Nuh-uh. No way. *Slow?* That meant traveling with Buster. Every rock or tree root presented an obstacle that we had to go around rather than over. Every hole, too. Our journey must have been lengthened by at least a third. And the extra length, given how slow we went, meant we traveled all through late afternoon and evening and straight into night. The whole time I had to be alert for enemies on the ground and in the air—extra alert because I was looking out not just for myself, but for Buster, too. Still, once I got him off the subject of mating, this old guy was some conversationalist.

For example, on the subject of spiders. The

grasses were loaded with spiders. We'd hop, and spiders would explode into frantic races in every direction. For me spiders had always been just a flavorful snack. But Buster studied them.

Oh, I wouldn't let him stop to examine them now, because it was getting dark fast. No, he had studied them back at his home. And he had discovered that spiders need air. They drown fast if you drag them underwater. But one kind of spider makes a bubble, and it can hang inside the bubble under the water. That was really cool to think about. As soon as all this stuff with Jimmy was past, I wanted to go searching in our pond for spiders in bubbles.

And that's not all we discussed. Buster was such an easy guy to talk with that I soon found myself telling him about Jimmy and the rest of the fawgs and Mamma and Pin and the people at the palace and everything—the whole story of why I was on this journey. And he listened. I liked him for that.

So I really couldn't complain about his slowness. Buster was good company.

Around the time when it got so dark I could hardly see my own feet, the air changed. It took on that fresh, light, moist feel that signaled a good-sized pond close by. Buster felt it, too, I knew, because he surged ahead.

I breathed in deep and let the treasured smell of

pond fill me. A mosquito went up my nose. I sucked it down into my mouth and swallowed; then I hopped after Buster, breathing shallowly.

Soon the ground turned to mud under my feet. Firm mud. Then easily molded mud. Then squishy, squashy, squooshy mud. I scanned everywhere for crocodile prints, but if there were any, they weren't at this end of the pond. So we slipped into the shallows in comradely silence and swam and glided and floated and swam again. Ah, the glory of water.

There were no croaks. All the other frogs were sleeping, of course. It was closer to dawn than dusk by now, we'd taken so long to get here.

All right, I'd made it this far. I had done the whole trip in one day and most of this night. With no sleep the night before. And with Buster lengthening the journey. I amazed even myself.

The prince's family palace was near this pond somewhere. Mamma said when I saw animals that looked like the prince's horse—only shorter and fatter and with horns—animals she called cows—then I'd know I was in the right place.

My task was to find Jimmy and bring him home.

If I could convince him.

Tomorrow would be the most important day of my life.

I left Buster asleep, burrowed into the soft bank—

after all, he was now as well off as he was going to be—and I nestled in among iris shoots. I slept hard.

"You wanted to see it," came a voice. "So here it is."

I woke with a start and slipped into the water. Humans were near. I came up cautiously, letting only my eyes and nostrils break the surface. The brightness of the sun stunned me. It was already a quarter of the way across the sky. I'd never slept this late before.

The prince and two other men walked on the shore. One was old and stooped. The other was young like the prince, but, in a strange way, handsome. He walked finely, with his knees pointed slightly outward, and the skin on his face and hands glowed a delicate hint of green.

I swam closer to the bank.

"Well," said the prince, "let's swim. What do you say, Father?" He stopped and pulled off his shirt.

"Help me," said the old king, tugging at his own shirt.

Meanwhile, the attractive young fellow stripped off his clothes in a flash and eased into the pond as though he belonged there. He cut the water cleanly, leaving hardly a ripple behind. A fine swimmer, that one. And, oh dear, he was coming my way.

I swam back to the irises and hid.

The prince slid into the water now, too, and he was also quite a swimmer. These humans really knew how to get around in water. I hadn't expected that, given how oddly they traveled on land.

Finally, the prince's father jumped in. But he splashed like a dying duck, flapping his arms every which way and kicking his legs one at a time. He was drowning, and the young men didn't even seem to notice.

But now the old king called out, "Marvelous, isn't it? When your mother and I were young, we used to come skinny-dipping here together." He laughed raucously.

So that ridiculous performance was his idea of swimming. Disgraceful. And now he was floating on his back. Absurd.

The young men floated near the iris, just a leap away from me, but far from the prince's father. And they, at least, floated normally, with their heads bobbing above water and the rest of them hanging below.

"I'm so glad you came back," whispered the prince. "But how did you manage it without the help of the ring?"

"Thally kithed me," said the young fellow.

What a funny way he talked—it was sort of like how the performers talked at a Pin Impersonator Festival—but different, too.

"Sally kissed you, and you turned into a human," said the prince. "Just like last summer. Why did she do it this time?"

"I tricked her into it. I pretended I had a boo-boo."

"She kissed your boo-boo?"

"Mmm-hmm. Then thee thcreamed."

"She screamed?" said the prince.

I felt like screaming. This conversation was weird. Had the prince actually said Sally's kiss had turned this man into a human? What was he before the kiss?

"Mmm-hmm. Thee had no idea where I came from."

And now I recognized the way he talked. Why, this fellow was the kitchen boy from last summer. The one called Thimmy. No one else talked that way. At last something was as it should be: Thimmy had been a boy last summer, so it was normal that he had grown into a young adult by now, not like Sally or the prince or the rest of these humans, who had barely aged at all.

The prince laughed and swam closer to Thimmy. "We're going to have so much fun together," he whispered. "Let's talk about your new life."

I hopped to the top of the iris shoots to hear better. The view was good up here. I scouted the area. Not a single frog in sight. How strange.

"Not yet," said Thimmy. He took a gulp of water, then spit it out in a long stream that arced practically to the bank. "We have a problem firth. The hag ith back."

"The hag?" The prince's voice rose in surprise. "She's back?"

I was just as surprised. How did Thimmy find out?

"How?" said the prince. "She was a rock."

"Thally turned her into a crocodile with the ring."

"The hag's magic ring?"

Thimmy nodded.

"You mean Sally stole it from me again?" said the prince. "This is terrible." He moved his arms back and forth, treading water in excitement. "She kept saying it was only fair that she should get it, since Marissa got a wedding ring. So I hid it really well— for her own protection. And she found it anyway." His arms were going so fast now, the air was full of splashes. "But how did she learn what to do with it? She didn't even know it was magic. She had no idea it could transform things."

"Right. It happened by acthident. Thally rubbed the ring and then withed the hag-rock would become a crocodile."

"She wished for a crocodile, and, boom, just like

that, there was a crocodile. Yes, I can imagine the whole scene." The prince went underwater, then popped up, spitting water in his excitement. He shook his head wildly. "That means the crocodile will come after Sally to get the ring back."

"Right. We have to get it from her firtht."

"Not we—me," said the prince. "I'll get the ring, and I'll take care of the hag for good. You stay out of it. I mean that."

"I can't," said Thimmy. "I need to help."

"You're finally here—alive and well—let's keep it that way."

"The pond ith my rethponthibility," said Thimmy.

The prince's face softened a little. "In some ways the pond is more your responsibility than mine. You're right. Sally's nothing but a little trouble-maker, though. I know how to handle her, and you don't. So let me take care of the Sally part."

"All right," said Thimmy.

"Good. For the moment, anyway, Sally and the ring are in my father's palace, safe from the hag. So we can take a little time to talk. I'm glad you're here. You listened to me the last time I came to your pond, didn't you? You made the right choice."

"I haven't really made my thoithe yet, Daddy."
Daddy?

"Then let me help you make it," said the prince. "I love you. I have always loved you. I can offer you a good life. Stay a human, my son. Live in the palace with me forever."

Stay a human? But what else would he have been? My head spun. I couldn't afford to miss a single word. I jumped off the iris leaves into the water and swam up right behind Thimmy.

"Would it have to be forever?" said Thimmy. "With the ring, I can go back and forth whenever I want."

"True." The prince furrowed his brow. "But just look how old you got by spending this past year in the pond. If you spend another one, by the time you come to me again next summer, you'll be middle-aged. Think how much of your life you already gave up. How much more do you want to waste?"

Thimmy spit a long arc again. "The pond ith a good home," he said loudly. "I love it. I love frogth."

"So do I," said the prince in a hushed voice. "But there are good times ahead as a human. And if I had stayed Pin, I might have been eaten by now."

At that, I gulped so much water, I choked.

"Did you hear something?" asked the prince.

"Thutht barely."

"It's almost mealtime," called the prince's father. He stood on the bank dripping. "You fellows should get dressed and start the long walk home. I have something I want to do, a little surprise, you might say; then I'll follow at my own pace."

"We're going, Father, in just one minute." The prince moved very close to Thimmy and whispered, "Choose the life of a man. You could marry a beautiful princess. You could travel the world. You could see things you've never imagined, experience things that go far beyond anything a frog could ever dream."

With those words I fainted dead away.

TWELVE

Thimmy

A FROG WHO faints in water dies.

I wasn't dead, though. The mud under my belly told me that much. I coughed. Water came whooshing out my mouth and nose. I pulled myself into a squat and blinked.

Buster blinked back at me.

"Did you save me?" I asked, which was a dumb question, since there was no one else who could have done it. He must have been following me around since last night. Funny old guy. "Thanks."

"Anytime," said Buster. "It was fun." He hesitated. "At least it got fun when you turned out to be alive."

His voice was sincere but weak. It must have

been hard for him to drag me up onto the bank, given his bad leg and how old he was. "I owe you one," I said.

"You brought me here," said Buster. "You were right: My pond had shrunk to a mud hole. When it rains hard and long, I can go back home. But till then, I'm better off here. No doubt about that. None at all. So we're even. I haven't met anyone yet. The frogs here must be late coming out of hibernation. But I know I will soon enough. This is a big pond."

I was glad to see that Buster really was a thoughtful frog, because right now I needed someone to help me think. I looked around. "Are the humans gone?"

"Yes."

"Did you hear what they said?" I asked.

"Every word," said Buster.

"What did you understand from it?"

"Junk," said Buster. "Balderdash. Pure gibberish. One of them claimed he used to be Pin, the very Pin that's a legend in all the ponds around here, the very Pin you told me fathered Jimmy and the rest of the fawgs."

"Right. That one's the prince."

"Are all humans that berserk?" asked Buster.

I thought about Sally. She was the human I'd had the most contact with. "I think so."

"Pity," said Buster. "They could be interesting creatures if they had better brains."

Who could disagree with that? "Listen, Buster, there's a puzzle here."

Buster waited.

"Humans age more slowly than frogs," I said. "This much I've figured out. It's not an illness; that's just how it works. Somehow the prince blames that fact on the pond. He said that Thimmy . . ."

"Who's Thimmy?" asked Buster.

"The young fellow who was swimming with the prince. The prince said Thimmy had spent the past year in the pond and had wasted years of his human life."

A fly circled over Buster's head. He glanced up at it, then looked down at the mud. Why, he didn't even have the energy left to catch a snack.

I remembered when Mamma tossed me a water strider, just two days ago. It seemed ages, so much had happened since then. I missed Mamma a lot.

And I missed Jimmy.

I zapped the fly out of the air and tossed it to Buster.

Buster caught it on the tip of his tongue. "Thankth," he said with his tongue still out. Then he snapped in his tongue and swallowed.

Thankth. That's the way Thimmy talked.

And what had Thimmy said? "Thutht barely."
And he meant "just barely."

Thutht. Just.

Thimmy. Jimmy.

I sneezed uncontrollably, then had to turn in a circle to stop myself.

Buster hopped beside me. "Are you sick?"

"I'm thinking."

Last summer Thimmy was a boy, and now he was an adult. The other humans had barely aged. But Thimmy had aged in one year as much as a frog ages in one year.

And the prince said Thimmy had visited him last summer and then spent the past year in the pond.

Jimmy had visited the palace last summer. And Jimmy had spent the past year in the pond.

And, most of all, Jimmy had told me he was the palace kitchen boy. That's exactly what he had said.

I was getting dizzy. "If a frog can turn into a human . . ."

"Frogs can't turn into humans," said Buster.

"The prince said he used to be Pin. If that were true . . ."

"That's not true," said Buster.

"Stop interrupting me." I sneezed. "Now, if it went both ways—frogs into humans and humans into frogs—then Thimmy and Pin could go back and forth—frog, human, frog, human. But when they were frogs, they'd age fast like other frogs; and when they were human, they'd age slow like other humans."

"You sound as berserk as the prince," said Buster.

"I'm finally making sense. I've figured out Thimmy-Jimmy."

"Who's Thimmy-Jimmy?" said Buster.

"Jimmy."

Buster looked bewildered. "Jimmy is Thimmy-Jimmy?"

"Yes."

"Are you Thracie-Gracie and am I Thuster-Buster?"

"Of course not. And you know what else? Thimmy is Thimmy-Jimmy."

"You just said Jimmy was Thimmy-Jimmy."

"Right."

"Wait a minute," said Buster. "That means Jimmy is Thimmy. And that can't be. Thimmy is that human, and Jimmy is a frog."

"Precisely." It was growing clearer every moment. "I have to get to Thimmy-Jimmy, the human, and convince him to turn back into a frog and come home to our pond before the prince convinces him to stay a human forever."

"More and more berserk," said Buster. "Cripes! Look at that!"

I followed his eyes.

Two big humps appeared out of the water, then two smaller ones appeared in front of them. The back humps opened to reveal the vertical slits of reptile eyes. The front humps were nostrils. The crocodile glided through the water straight toward us. That's why I hadn't heard any frogs last night or seen any this morning. That's why Buster hadn't met any yet. The hag-croc had been feeding on the frogs in this pond, and those that remained were deep in hiding.

I nudged Buster. "Come on! Fast!"

Wop!

A net came down over Buster and me.

I hopped like an idiot and wound up on my side, tangled tight. Buster was sensible enough not to move.

"Got you!" shouted the prince's old father. "Two in one net. I'm so glad I thought to bring it. I don't know where all the other frogs have gone, but at least my son's friend can have a little appetizer before lunch." He twisted the net and lifted us into the air. "Look at those nice plump legs."

Then he fell. "Ack!" he screamed.

The hag-croc had him by the leg and was dragging him toward the water.

"Ahhhh!" screamed the king. He thrashed and kicked and hit the croc on the head with the net.

Buster and I got slung around, bang, boom. Finally, we were flung free, through the air, plop, into the water. I surfaced as fast as I could.

The croc was totally underwater by now, and the king was shouting, "Help! Save me! Help!" But there was no one around to hear—no one but us. The croc rolled on the bottom while the king flailed above, his arms spinning round and round. That couldn't last. Either the croc would figure out she had to go to a deeper part of the pond, or the king would get too tired to struggle. One way or the other, the old king would soon be underwater, too.

I don't know that much about humans, but anyone knows that land creatures won't last long underwater.

Still, what could I do? What could any frog do?

There was no way to take the croc's attention from the old king.

Or maybe there was.

I looked around. Sure enough, Buster was right behind me. "Get the king's attention," I said, "so he'll keep his head above water."

"How?" said Buster. "A croc's got him by the leg. That's all he cares about."

"Just do something amazing. Hurry."

"I guess I could tell him about spiders."

"Sure. And, whatever you do, stay out of the croc's way. Have a good life, Buster." And I swam straight for the croc.

She had stopped rolling and was resting on the bottom, with the king's leg secure in her mouth, waiting for him to give up, sink under, and drown, so she could rip him to pieces. Her eyes were shuttered tight. I took a lesson from Jimmy and swam fast, ramming my head into the croc's spongy eyeball.

Her eyelids popped open.

"I've got the ring," I lied.

Her eyes bulged.

"Your crystal ring," I said. "I've got it in my mouth—just like last summer, you old hag." And I swam away like crazy.

THIRTEEN

Legs

THE CROC CAME after me, just as I'd hoped. But she came faster than I expected. She didn't glide; she swam. My only chance was to get out of the water, where she couldn't move so easily.

I climbed onto the mud bank and hopped pell-mell.

But she was right behind me, snapping at my heels. How on earth? She had a wide belly, stumpy legs, and she wiggled maniacally as she ran, so she should have been slow. But somehow she had lifted her middle up, and she was zooming after me.

I hopped zig, I hopped zag, I hopped zig zag zig.

The croc ran zig, she ran zag, she ran zig zag zig.

Every change of direction slowed her down. But not enough. I was tiring fast.

Then I saw it. A short, fat horse with horns: a cow. I leaped as high as I could and landed on the ridge above the cow's eyes. Then I clamped my legs around a horn as she took off, mooing, with the croc right behind.

We loped across a meadow. The croc ran behind, and cows scattered ahead. We loped back across the meadow. The croc ran back. The cows smashed into each other in noisy panic. We circled the meadow.

That croc had to be tired. This had been going on far too long now, and her legs were nothing compared to the cow's. She could never keep it up.

But somehow she did.

"Mrrraaah," came loud and harsh. I looked around. On the other side of a wood fence was a massive creature with giant horns. "Mrrraaah," said the creature.

"My bull," cried the cow whose horn I clung to. "Save me."

The bull glowered, and his nostrils flared. He pawed the ground and rushed at the fence. *Crack.* He burst through and charged.

"Criminy!" shouted the hag-croc. She turned tail and ran for the pond.

I dropped from the cow's horn. I was so dizzy, I had to sit still until the earth stopped moving. Then I hopped to the nearest fence and jumped up onto a post to survey the lay of the land.

The cows huddled together at one end of a watering hole. Their frazzled moos had turned to sporadic nervous lows. And between the lows I thought I heard an occasional croak. How could that be? But, there, I heard another. And another.

This had been a really rough day so far. I needed comfort, and nobody could blame me if I took a little time out to spend in the soothing company of other frogs. I leaped from the post into a ditch that ran along the fence line.

I hopped along and, whoa, what was that figure all curled up ahead in the ditch?

The figure saw me at just about the same moment. "My froggy! Whoopee!" Sally sprang at me, hands open.

In my surprise, I hopped straight up and came down on her head. I was about to hop again when suddenly it was all dark, and I couldn't see a thing.

"Hey, under there, froggy in my bonnet, I'm glad you came back."

So she'd flipped her bonnet over me; I was Sally's prisoner again. This was getting to be a habit. A bad habit.

She whisked off her bonnet, me in it, and crumpled it like a sack. Then she looked down through the opening at me. "What are you doing out here? Were you following me?" She narrowed her eyes. "Oooo, how strange you are. Sometimes you're big, and sometimes you're not. When I first caught you, you were pixie. Then when you rode with me in the coach, you were big. And now you're pixie again. You're a blow-up froggy, aren't you? I've heard about that kind of frog. You blow up when you're afraid, right?"

I'd never met such a brainless creature in my life. She was dumber than the smallest minnow.

"Well, I guess we have to go home now and face stupid Prince Know-It-All. He wants my ring. *Mine!* The hog. He has tons of jewelry, and he wants to take my ring. So I came out here to plan something mean to do to him." She screwed up her face into a monster grimace. "That's when I saw the croc racing around, and I got so flustered, I hid in this ditch." She laughed. "That was pretty dumb, wasn't it? Crocodiles must like ditches." She stood up and scouted the area. "The croc's still out of sight. Double whoopee. Let's go." Sally tied her bonnet closed and ran, swinging me around like crazy.

Moments later she reached into the bonnet and pulled me out, then burst into the palace kitchen.

A woman was chopping plants on a board. Pungent odors filled the room. "Ah, there you are. And with another frog. Why, Mistress Sally, have you been at it, too? You shouldn't have gone out alone like that. The prince has been looking for you everywhere. He went riding off on his horse to find you, and he was worried something awful."

Sally frowned and stuck out the arm that held me. "Take care of my frog, Bertha. I have to go tell the guards to catch a crocodile."

Bertha took me without even a second glance. "The monster put twenty-two holes in the king's leg, it did. The guards are fixing to hunt it down."

"But they mustn't kill it," said Sally.

"Don't be silly, Miss. A crocodile is dangerous."

"But it's mine," shouted Sally. She ran out of the kitchen, shouting, "Mine, mine."

Bertha gave a loud sigh and shook her head. "Ah, well. One more frog." She spun around and dropped me.

I fell, splat, on top of another frog. And another and another and another. I was in an enormous bucket with countless other frogs.

"What's going on?" I asked.

No one answered. Frogs tend to go silent in the face of danger.

"Come on," I said, "tell me what's happening."

"Are you dumb?"

I stared. But it wasn't Jimmy. "Anything but," I said firmly.

"We're about to be eaten," came a voice.

"Our legs, at least," said another.

"They're making a feast for some frog-eating guest."

"Hi," came a voice from near the bottom—weak but familiar.

"Buster? Is that you?"

"That's me," said Buster. "After the king crawled out of the pond, I hopped off, looking for you. And then I saw a watering hole and I just knew there were froggies there. So I went right for it. But the king was behind me. He swooped me up and limped home. Then he ordered a guard to go back and catch more frogs."

"So you're the one who led him to us," said the frog right under me. "Traitor."

"It's not Buster's fault," I said. "No sensible frog would be in that watering hole anyway."

"Watch your words, stranger. We're sensible enough to get out of the big pond when a croc comes."

"The croc, yeah, the croc," came voices from under me.

"That crocodile's the cause of all our problems,"

said the frog to my left. "If it hadn't been for the croc, we wouldn't have clustered at the cows' watering hole, and the guard couldn't have caught so many of us so fast."

The rightness of those words hung in the air. No one said anything else.

We sat motionless and listened to Bertha chopping greens to cook with our legs. The sharp smells prickled my nose.

The frog to my right moaned. The frog under me hiccuped. The frog in front of me let out gas. Gradually everyone started making their own little tics. Our froggy brains were coming unraveled.

This is how Jimmy must have felt when he was trapped in the hag's bucket. But Jimmy got free because the other fawgs threw themselves against the side and tipped it over.

"A nice bit of olive oil to fry up those legs in," came Bertha's voice. "Ah, this is going to be scrumptious." The sound of sizzling oil stopped all our tics. The whole bucket of frogs sat perfectly still. Doomed.

No fawgs to help us. No fawgs.

Only frogs.

Oh, yes. Frogs. There were all of us in this bucket. Frogs and frogs and frogs.

"If fawgs can do it, frogs can do it," I said.

"What?" came a voice from below.

"Everybody move toward the side of the bucket away from the noise of the stove," I said.

"How will that help?" asked a frog beside me.

"Yeah," said another, "she can reach us anywhere we go in this bucket."

"Just do it," said Buster.

Good old Buster.

"On the count of three," I said. "One, two . . ."

The frogs scrambled over each other, not even waiting for "three." Panicked frogs act no better than tadpoles.

The bucket teetered, then tipped. Slam.

Frogs hopped free and wild-eyed.

"Frogs!" shouted Bertha. "Get back in that bucket."

Frogs were under the table, and on top of barrels, and banging against the walls.

"Go for the windows," I yelled. "Those holes up there."

"Frogs?" Marissa, the princess wife of the prince, came running into the kitchen. "Did you shout frogs?" She gaped at the scene. "What are all these frogs doing here?"

"That's our meal," shouted the prince's old father, stumbling in with one leg bandaged in white cloth. "Quick, catch them. Close the shutters."

Frogs were hopping from the floor, to a chair, to the window ledge, and flying off and away to freedom. I myself balanced on the window ledge. But then I looked back and saw Buster still on the floor by the bucket. He was a goner for sure. It didn't make sense, but I hopped down and went to him.

"Let them go," said Marissa, holding her arms in close to her chest as though she were afraid of us. "You know how the prince feels about frogs. He thinks they're all wonderful."

"The prince isn't even here. He's off somewhere looking for Sally."

"He'll come back," said Marissa, "and he'll be horrified if you made frogs for lunch."

"No, he won't. His friend loves frogs," said the prince's father. "I heard him say that out at the pond."

"I love them alive," said Thimmy-Jimmy, coming up behind them. "Not to eat." He knelt down beside Buster and me. "Go on, old guy."

Buster just sat there.

Thimmy-Jimmy gave him a little shove.

Buster made a hobbly hop.

"Uh-oh," said Thimmy-Jimmy. "Look at the thcratch on that leg." He put his face down to Buster's scratched leg. "Poor old guy. I'll try to help that leg of yourth. But firtht wait till I get your little friend here moving." He turned to me now and carefully scooped me up. His eyes grew huge. "Grathie."

I sat in his hand. Thimmy-Jimmy's hand.

Which meant Jimmy's hand.

That Jimmy had a hand was amazing enough. But that I was actually in it was incomprehensible. And I realized I'd been in it before—for I had sat in Thimmy's hand last summer.

The unbelievable was happening.

FOURTEEN

The Choice

MY SHOCK LEFT me speechless through much that followed. But once it wore off, panic set in. "You should have jumped somewhere. Under the table. Anywhere." I hopped over Buster's head and landed on the other side of him. Then I hopped back. We were in a tall container that the cook called a basket. The cook had whisked me off Thimmy-Jimmy's hand and grabbed Buster, too, and put us in here. I heard Thimmy-Jimmy make her promise to keep us safe until he came back. But what good was that? This cook fried frogs. And there was hardly any room inside here at all, except above our heads, so I'd been doing the highest jumps ever. "You should have," I said for the twentieth time.

"You really should have. Then we'd both be free now."

"Don't talk," said Buster.

"I have to talk. Look what you did."

"I was tired and injured and, most of all, scared," said Buster. "First, you went off with a crocodile chasing you, and I thought you were dead. Then a human caught me—for the second time—then another one touched me. So shut up."

I sat there. "You didn't have to get mean," I said at last.

"Apparently I did," said Buster.

"I just don't want to have to take care of you," I said. "It's all I can do to take care of myself." Then I remembered how Buster had saved me from drowning. I waited for him to bring that up. He didn't. He really was a nice guy. Finally, I said, "Sorry."

Then it rained, in a sweet burst.

"My old pond must be coming back to life right now," said Buster dreamily.

But the rain stopped. Just like that. It ceased.

I looked up.

Sally stared down at us. She held a funny-shaped bucket. Then she tilted it and water sprinkled out again. "You're mine," Sally whispered. "And don't you forget it. They're going to kill my crocodile, no matter what I say, so all I have left is the two of you. Thank goodness the prince's dumbbell friend decided to keep at least two frogs. He says you're a boy and a girl. I know what that means: You can make lots of babies and fill my moat. You just have to get well first. Let me see that boo-boo leg. I'll kiss it and make it better." She reached down for Buster.

Kiss? No! Not after the prince had said Sally's kiss turned a frog into a human. I had to save Buster.

I jumped into Sally's hand and squeezed my eyes shut against the horrible thought that she'd kiss me instead, and I'd become human.

"I wasn't reaching for you," whispered Sally. "I was reaching for the hurt one. But goody, you're friendly. And, oh, you're the one that jumped into my hand back at my palace, aren't you? And you jumped onto my head in the ditch. Ha! I tamed you."

Tame? Me? I opened my eyes. I'd never been so insulted in my life.

Sally brought me up level with her face. A string circled her neck. And I bet the crystal ring was hanging from it just inside the collar of her dress. "You're the croaky froggy, but for now, you have to be very quiet. Stubborn Prince-Know-It-All is still out somewhere on his horse looking for me, but now I'm hiding from his dumbbell friend. He said he needed to talk to me. He said you don't belong to me. Imagine, talking to a princess like that. I think he wants you two for himself. But I'll never let you go."

"Oh, yeth you will." Thimmy-Jimmy came into the room.

Sally spun around. "Stop right there and tell me what you call Prince-Know-It-All," she said imperiously.

This sounded suspicious to me. "Don't do it, Thimmy-Jimmy," I called. "It's a trap."

"You recognithe me?" said Thimmy-Jimmy.

"What an idiotic question," said Sally.

"I wathn't talking to you," said Thimmy-Jimmy. "I wath talking to her." He pointed at me.

"You were talking to my frog? Don't you dare bother my frog. It is mine, you know, mine mine mine."

"Get us out of here," I screamed at Thimmy-Jimmy.

"Stop that croaking," Sally said to me. "Say it right now," she said to Thimmy-Jimmy, "say that word you call the prince. And don't think that because you're an adult, you don't have to obey me. I'm royalty. Besides, if you don't, I'll plow into you and knock you flat."

Thimmy-Jimmy jumped backward in alarm. "Pin," he said weakly.

"And how do you say 'mince'?"

"What?" said Thimmy-Jimmy.

"You heard me," said Sally. "Mince. Like what Bertha does to the spices. Mince mince mince. Like what I'm going to do to you if you don't answer me."

"Minth," said Thimmy-Jimmy.

"Ha! I've caught you. You talk the stupidest way. Just like the kitchen boy last summer."

"Mmm-hmm. We're the thame perthon."

"You're the same person? That's impossible. You're much older than him," said Sally. "But there's one thing the two of you have in common: You're both fakes."

Thimmy-Jimmy winced.

So Sally knew about Thimmy-Jimmy's double life, too. "Grab it, Thimmy-Jimmy," I yelled. "Grab it and grab us and run!"

"Grab what?" said Thimmy-Jimmy.

"Hush, froggy. Your noise is annoying." With her free hand, Sally clamped my mouth shut. "And what are you talking about?" she said to Thimmy-Jimmy.

"Nothing." Thimmy-Jimmy looked at me.

I looked at Sally's neck, where the crystal ring hung, hoping his eyes would follow my gaze. But he just looked desperately at my face.

"Okay," said Sally, "admit it. Admit you do that

stupid talk on purpose. Your tongue is not deformed."

Thimmy-Jimmy looked startled. "Deformed?"

"Don't act so innocent. That's what you're pretending to have. A deformed tongue. I heard the prince explaining it to his father yesterday. You fooled him."

"Ah," said Thimmy-Jimmy, in a relieved sigh. "That'th what you mean by fake."

"Stop it! Don't say things like 'that'th.' You can't fool me. I've been thinking about how you talk, and if you really have a deformed tongue, you should say 'printh' not 'pin.' Just like you say 'minth' for 'mince.' That's exactly what you should say: printh, printh, printh."

"Pin ith what the printh callth himthelf."

"What? The prince doesn't call himself Pin."

"He doeth when he'th a fawg."

"A fawg? What stupid word are you saying wrong now? Besides, it's 'the prince' not simply 'prince' or 'printh' or 'pin.'"

"Right," said Thimmy-Jimmy, "de fawg Pin. But he callth himthelf Pin for thort."

"He calls himself Pin for short? That's pure stupid." Sally frowned. "And you can't trick me."

"I'm not trying to trick anyone," said Thimmy-Jimmy.

Sally lifted an eyebrow. "Oh yeah? Prove it. Answer my questions. And if you don't tell the truth, I'll know it, and I'll get you locked up. That means prison. Understand?"

"Yeth."

"The word is 'yes,' so stop with the fake 'yeth' right now. Question number one: What are you doing here?"

I tensed up. Now that the king's men were going to kill the hag-croc, why was Thimmy-Jimmy still hanging around the palace? Sally had asked exactly what I wanted to know.

"Making a thoithe."

"It's 'choice,' not 'thoithe.' I'm sick of that game. Talk right."

"I have to thoothe . . ."

Sally tapped her shoe impatiently. "'Choose' . . . say 'choose.' Your fake talk makes me mad."

". . . whether I want to be a man or a fawg."

"I told you, I never heard of a fawg."

"It'th a thpethial kind of frog," said Thimmy-Jimmy.

"A special kind of frog." Sally gaped. Then she licked her bottom lip. "Liar. Question number two: Where did you come from?"

"The pond near your palathe. But I hatthed in your well."

"Hatthed?"

"You know. Born from an egg."

"You hatched?" Sally frowned. "What junk."

"I'm a fawg," said Thimmy-Jimmy.

"Double liar. Question number three: How come the prince likes you so much?"

"He'th my father."

"Ha! I caught you in your own lie." Sally stomped both feet. "If the prince is a man, and you're a fawg, how can he be your father?"

"A magic ring turned him into a fawg. And then, oh, it'th a long thtory."

"I don't want to hear your long story," said Sally. "Triple liar. The next thing you'll say is that the ring turned you into a man."

"No, you turned me into a man. You kithed me."

"I kithed you? Oh, I kissed you. What? I never kissed you. How dare you say such a thing."

"You kithed me when I was a fawg."

Sally twisted her mouth and pulled her eyebrows together.

"You know," said Thimmy-Jimmy. "Yethterday."

"Oh. You saw me kiss that frog yesterday."

"That wath me. That'th why I appeared right then and made you thream."

"You did appear suddenly," said Sally in a sick voice. "You did make me scream." Her hand shook.

"So you're saying my kiss can turn a frog into a man?"

"Mmm-hmm."

Sally looked at me. Then she looked at Thimmy-Jimmy. Her eyes glazed over. "You really believe you are the same kind of creature as this thing in my hand?"

"Mmm-hmm," said Thimmy-Jimmy. "That'th Grathie. Give her to me, pleath." He reached for me.

Sally quickly dropped me in his hand and backed away. "I don't know how you managed to be there right when I kissed the frog yesterday. But I know something without a doubt: You should be locked up for real," she said. "It's not your tongue that's deformed; it's your brain. You've got bats in your belfry. You're one hundred percent fried. You're crazy. Mad. Insane. Bonkers."

"The ring is around her neck," I shouted. "Grab it."

Thimmy-Jimmy's eyes opened wide. He leaped at Sally, grabbing for her neck.

"Help! Murder!" screamed Sally.

The string broke, the ring fell—*clink*—on the floor.

As Thimmy-Jimmy's hand closed around it, Sally ran screaming from the room.

"Choose right now," I said to Thimmy-Jimmy,

"before they come to lock you up. Do you want to be a fawg or a man?"

"How do you know about everything?" asked Thimmy-Jimmy.

"I'm not dumb. Hurry."

"You're thmart. I alwayth knew that. Did you hop all the way here to find me?" he asked.

"Yes."

"Why?"

"You can't ask a question like that," I said. "Anyway, it's my turn to ask." I gathered all my courage. "How come you haven't chosen a partner yet?"

Thimmy-Jimmy took a deep breath. "You onth thaid that my thtorieth about the palathe were crathy."

"I said your palace stories were the craziest of all your stories, to be exact."

"Do you thtill think that?"

I thought about princess kisses and crystal rings. Those things were so hard to understand. But then I thought about how I'd bonked the hag-croc in the eye and saved the old king's life. Just with my wits. And I thought about how the frogs in the kitchen bucket had leaped to one side and made it tip over. Just by working together. So many things were possible. "No." I shook my head hard. "I believe every word you've ever said."

"You believe in me."

That wasn't exactly what I'd said. But it was true. "I believe in you."

Thimmy-Jimmy grinned. He held up the hag's crystal ring. "Humanth live a lot longer than frogth. They can do lotth and lotth of thingth that frogth can't do. Would you like to be a human, Grathie?"

"Never," I said.

"I didn't think tho." Thimmy-Jimmy rubbed the ring hard until it glowed.

He was about to make a wish. And there's only one wish that he could be making right now. Happiness made the skin all over my body tingle. But, oh, what about Buster? "Wait," I said. "Knock the basket over first so Buster can be free."

"Ith that hith name?" Thimmy-Jimmy looked down into the basket. "Pleathed to meet you, Buthter."

"Likewise," said Buster. That frog sure could keep his cool.

"Ith he your . . . friend?" asked Thimmy-Jimmy. And the way he said it, I knew what he was asking.

"He's my friend, yes. His pond dried to a mud hole, and he's coming to live in our pond." I looked down at Buster to see his reaction to my words, given that we'd never talked about this before.

Buster, however, was looking discreetly down at his own toes.

Thimmy-Jimmy tipped over the basket, and Buster hopped out. Thimmy-Jimmy looked at the ring again. It still glowed, as though it was waiting for his wish. He hesitated. Then he put it in his pocket.

Without wishing.

He would stay a man.

My throat got thick, and my head filled with buzzing. I couldn't even look at him now; I hung my head.

"I wathn't thinking right," said Thimmy-Jimmy softly. "I could have made a big mithtake. There'th thomething important I have to do firth—thomeone I love that I have to talk to."

FIFTEEN

The Puddle

WHO DID THIMMY-JIMMY love? It was hard to keep that question from popping from my mouth as we sneaked quickly through the palace halls till Thimmy-Jimmy stopped in front of a shut door. He looked at me in one hand and Buster in the other; then he knocked on the door with his forehead.

No one answered.

Thimmy-Jimmy shook his head sadly. "Pin ith thtill out on his horthe looking for Thally. We'll have to wait."

Oh, that's who he loved. I sighed in relief. But then my heart clutched. "Sally will come with the guards and have you thrown in prison. And she'll capture Buster and me. We should leave right away."

"But what about the croc? If we take the ring to the pond, how will Pin get it back?" Thimmy-Jimmy jumped in place. "All right, I've got it. We'll go to the pond. I'll be a man till we get there becauthe it'th a long way. We'll go a lot fathter with me carrying you in my handth than if we all hop the whole way. Then, after I tranthform, I'll hide the ring till Pin cometh to find me." His voice shook with worry. "He'll come, I know," he said hopefully.

I remembered the conversation in the pond between Thimmy-Jimmy and his father. I remembered how the prince said he loved Thimmy-Jimmy. "Yes, he'll come."

I quickly found out that Thimmy-Jimmy had a nice way of traveling. It was a combination of a human run and a frog leap, and it took my breath away. We passed Buster's mud hole, which was even drier today, then loped through the meadow of flowers and grasses. We crossed the bridge over the brook and zoomed through the woods. It wasn't even twilight when I smelled our giant pond and heard the familiar croaks.

Thimmy-Jimmy sighed with satisfaction. He set Buster on the bank and wiped off his forehead. His body in human form made its own water, which dripped down the sides of his face and wet his shirt in front and back. "Home," he said, digging his toes into the mud.

Buster hopped immediately into the water. "Not bad," he said, swimming happily in and out of the lily pads. "Not bad at all."

Thimmy-Jimmy took the ring out of his pocket. "We have to hide the ring until Pin can come for it."

"Right," I said. "Make your wish. Then let's bury it."

That's when we heard hoofbeats.

"Hurry," I said.

"But it mutht be Pin. Who elthe would know where I went?" Thimmy-Jimmy clutched the ring and looked toward the direction the noise was coming from. "I can put the ring in hith hand."

He was right; the prince came riding toward us on Chester. Suddenly I didn't want Thimmy-Jimmy to put the ring in Pin's hand. I remembered that pond conversation too well; I didn't want Pin to have another chance to convince my Thimmy-Jimmy to stay a man. "No. Use the ring fast, and let's get in the water and hide."

"Not yet," said Thimmy-Jimmy.

"Where's the ring?" Pin came up and dismounted. "Sally's running around screaming that you're crazy and you attacked her and stole it." He grinned. "Good work."

"I'll give it to you in a minute," said Thimmy-Jimmy. I could sense his body tightening. "I want you to meet thomeone, Daddy." He held me out. "You met her before, a year ago, but you didn't know her name. Thith ith Grathie."

"Gracie? Nice to meet you, Gracie. And who's that other fellow in the water there?"

"He'th Buthter. He'th good, too. But Grathie ith the one I wanted you to know."

The prince looked at Thimmy-Jimmy. His eyes slowly widened with understanding. "Is she . . . your Jade?"

"Yeth. I brought her home."

"But wait, Jimmy. Don't let her go. We can change Gracie into a human. We can change any frogs you want to change. We can transform the whole pond if you want."

"What good ith life for a frog in a human body?"

The prince's eyes filled with tears. "You're right, of course," he said slowly. "It's good that you know when to say good-bye. Your Gracie would be no happier in a human body than my Jade would have been."

"I'm a frog in a human body, Daddy."

The prince looked stricken. I'd never seen such a sad face. "You're a fawg, Jimmy, not a frog. There's a difference. There's a human part to you."

"I have to tranthform. Good-bye, Daddy." Thimmy-Jimmy hugged the prince, careful not to squish me in the process.

The prince pulled back and put his hands on Thimmy-Jimmy's cheeks. "Don't disappear. Please. I can't bear losing you again."

"You'll alwayth know where I am, Daddy."

"You're right." The tears rolled down his cheeks now. "I wish you all good things, my child."

That's when another horse came into view. A pony.

"Thally," said Thimmy-Jimmy. "Oh, no."

"Stop, Freaky Foot," called Sally. "I followed your footprints. And you have a long fourth toe, just like that crazy kitchen boy did last summer. You really are him, aren't you? Somehow you got old. You didn't make the whole thing up. And you, you know-it-all prince, you're his father. You have to be nice to me from now on, or I'll tell Marissa."

Thimmy-Jimmy walked backward, rubbing the crystal ring.

"I understand the whole thing," said Sally. She rode her pony up between the prince and Thimmy-Jimmy. "That's the magic ring you talked about, isn't it? The one that turned the prince into a frog for a while. Or a fawg. Or whatever you called it.

That's why you grabbed it from my neck. But it's mine. Not the prince's. Mine! Give it back."

"Come on, ring," Thimmy-Jimmy said aloud, still walking backward. Then he stopped and looked at me with panic on his face. "Grathie, do I withh to become a fawg or a frog?"

"Does it matter?" I asked.

"It might."

"Just do something fast," I said.

Thimmy-Jimmy rubbed the ring and said, "Make me the right kind of amphibian for me, forever and ever."

Sally jumped off her horse. "Good. Then I get both you and that magic ring." She clapped her hands. "You can't possibly be as cute a fawg as that other pixie frog, but you'll be mine—forever—so that's good. Ack!" she screamed, as the prince grabbed her arms from behind.

"Don't interfere, Sally. And you don't want to touch that ring when a wish is in it."

"Wretched frog!" came a hateful screech.

It was the crocodile, puffing along straight at me. Oh, no, not one more creature to keep track of. All this was already too chaotic for my froggy brain to sort through.

"I've caught up to you at last," she shouted. "I'm

so sick of chasing everyone around on these awful short legs. Give me my ring, and I can run. I can even fly if I want. Give it to me, or I'll swallow you whole."

Sally screamed and pulled free of the prince. She ran for the willow tree.

"Stop, hag!" shouted the prince, jumping into the croc's path.

The croc opened her terrible jaws and swung her head from side to side, showing those gigantic teeth. "Get out of my way, you idiot. Don't you know I can snap you in half?"

"Hurry, Thimmy-Jimmy," I said, fighting every urge to flee. I wouldn't leave until he was with me.

Thimmy-Jimmy frantically rubbed the crystal ring. It finally glowed. That's when the croc saw the ring in his hand. "So you've got it now? You miserable man. It's mine!" she bellowed. She knocked the prince aside and ran right at Thimmy-Jimmy.

"Aiee!" he screamed as he fell backward over a rock. The ring flew through the air, tumbling golden in the sunlight, straight into the hag-croc's open mouth.

Thimmy-Jimmy disappeared, and Jimmy, my sweetest amphibian, sat on the mud. But a toad sat there, too, with the meanest-looking scowl I'd ever seen on any creature anywhere.

"What happened?" Sally called from the willow tree. "Where's that hateful crocodile? Where's my ring?"

She was right. Both the crocodile and ring had disappeared.

Sally dropped out of the tree.

Jimmy dove into the pond. I dove behind him.

"Gloom!" came the shriek.

"It's the hag," said Jimmy.

"It's the cry of a captured female toad," I said.

"Exactly. The crystal ring was still glowing when the hag-croc swallowed it. My wish was fresh in it. So the hag changed, too. Into the right kind of amphibian for her—a yucky toad. Forever. And the ring is someplace where it can never do harm again, stuck for good in her belly. Come on, let's go watch." Jimmy rose to the surface.

I rose with him.

Sally was already mounted on the pony again. She held the hag-toad in one hand and the reins in the other. "It would have been more fun with that ring," she said. "Then I could have turned anyone I didn't like into little creatures and kept them all in the moat. Ha! But at least I have you. You're a totally putrid-looking thing—but who cares? You're mine, all mine, and I'll never let you go. Whoopee!" She rode off.

The hag-toad's shriek faded in the distance.

Pin and Jimmy and I looked at each other and burst out laughing.

Then Pin got on Chester, gave a single wave good-bye, and followed Sally.

Jimmy sat in the mud, watching him leave.

They both knew this change was forever.

It was all too sad for me. I had to cheer Jimmy up. I did a flip in front of him.

"Croak."

I looked around.

That big male who had bothered me before was back. "Nice flip," he said. "You're good at flipping. I remember."

"She's with me," said Jimmy.

The male gave a puzzled "Croak." Then he took a second look at Jimmy. "Hey, I know you. Want to start another Pin Impersonator Festival? Now? Huh? Now?"

"Later," said Jimmy.

The male swam off haphazardly, muttering, "Later, later, all the time later."

"Welcome home, Jimmy and Gracie," called Mamma. She was sitting on a nearby rock. I was overjoyed to see her.

Jimmy hopped in a happy circle around me. "It's good to be me. It's good to be home."

That jumpy female who had been looking for Jimmy before came swimming up. "How about it, big boy?"

"He's with me," I said.

The female shrugged. "Who cares? There are tons of others. What about you?" she called to a male on a log.

The male slipped into the water, and they swam away together.

"Not much of a courtship," said Jimmy, looking after them.

"Frogs don't need much," said Mamma.

"That's true," said Buster, crawling up onto the rock and sitting right beside her. He gave a hopeful croak. "I'm Buster."

"Nice to meet you, Buster." Mamma ate a fly. "You seem like a nice sort. But I keep remembering Pin."

"Ah, Pin," said Buster. "I've heard about Pin." His voice was warm and sweet. "Every frog has."

I tensed up. Poor Mamma. Only now did I think about what all this meant to her. She had seen and heard everything that happened on the shore today. Buster might not have taken it all in, but I was sure Mamma had.

"Pin was like a dream," said Mamma. "Magic." She looked at the muddy bank. "The crocodile swallowed the hag's crystal ring," she said slowly. "So the magic is over. Pin will never come back now."

"He would be quite an act to follow," said Buster sadly.

"Yup," said Mamma. "But Pin didn't really belong to this world. He didn't really belong with me. Not like Jimmy belongs with Gracie."

Jimmy moved closer to me.

Buster brightened. "And repeat acts are never very good the second time around. A whole different show is better."

"Could be," said Mamma. She gave a sideways glance at Buster. "What kind of show can you put on?"

"I'm old," said Buster. "And I've got this bum leg. I guess just about all I can do well is talk."

"A little conversation can go a long way," said Mamma.

Buster hopped closer. "What do you know about spiders?"

We left them talking and swam away.

"There's a small pond not far from here," Jimmy said. "Well, actually, it's just a giant puddle. But it's bigger than the well I hatched in, and it has plenty of food. And it's not big enough for snakes or turtles. It would be a good place to keep an eye on tadpoles until they're old enough to fend for themselves." He swam under me and came up in front of my face. "It could be our puddle."

Keeping an eye on tadpoles—such an unfroglike idea. A fawg idea. A wonderful idea.

"And you could be the pixie of the puddle." He gave a single croak with his left vocal sac and charmed me completely.

"What are we waiting for?"